Ablazing Grace

FAITH AND FOILS

COZY MYSTERY SERIES #2

WENDY HEUVEL

Ablazing Grace

Chapter 1

Chatter and laughter echoed throughout the long church foyer as the after-service crowd discussed their Thanksgiving weekend plans while sipping their pumpkin spice lattes from the church café. Cassie Bridgestone craned her neck to see and admire the autumn displays of straw bales, pumpkins, and coloured leaves.

"Um... Cassie?"

She turned back to the handsome man in front of her. "Yes?"

Daniel Sawyer pointed at the paper cup of Earl Grey tea she grasped in front of her. "Your hair was in your tea."

A wet curl stuck to the sleeve of her fall cardigan. She sighed and rolled her eyes.

He gave her a smirk that lit up his blue eyes and made her stomach flip. "Do you want to fill out a thankful leaf with me?" Daniel pointed to a small group gathered around a table, writing things they were grateful for on paper leaves and sticking them to the thankful tree outlined on the wall.

"Sure." She followed Daniel to the tree, wondering what she should write on her leaf. What was she most thankful for this year? Her friendship with Daniel was a big thing, but that's all it was, and that's all she would let it be until he turned his life completely over to God. Grams had instilled in Cassie the importance of waiting for a man who loved God more than her, and her more than himself. Daniel had made steps in that direction, but he wasn't there yet, and she was growing rather impatient.

"Here." He handed her a red maple leaf cutout and a marker, and scribbled on his own yellow oak leaf.

Cassie set her tea on a windowsill, but before she could even take the top off her marker, Daniel had already taped his leaf to the tree. It had her name on it.

"You can't do that!" She felt the heat rush to her cheeks.

"Why not? I'm thankful for you."

Cassie swallowed to counter her dry throat. Now what? Did he expect her to put his name? She wanted to, but didn't want to give him the wrong impression. What else could she write? After a moment of deliberation, she wrote *friendships* on her leaf and grabbed a piece of tape to add it to the wall.

Daniel frowned but stayed silent.

"Have you seen Lexy?" Cassie opted to change the subject and glanced through the crowd, looking for her best friend. "I haven't talked to her yet this morning."

"Maybe Rick and Maggie have seen her." Daniel nodded his head in the opposite direction, where Cassie's brother and wife approached.

"Hey Cass!" Rick gave her a smile and shook hands with Daniel. "Daniel. Good to see you here."

Cassie gave Maggie a hug. "Hi! Where are the girls?" She loved her two nieces Olivia and Lily, ages eleven and seven respectively, and always looked forward to hugging them Sunday mornings.

"Running around somewhere, as usual." Maggie grinned.

Cassie studied Maggie's smiling face. "What's up?"

"Roberta has the flu."

"And that makes you happy?" She grabbed her tea from the sill and took a sip.

"She can't go to the women's group leadership conference, so they've asked me to go in her place!" Maggie's brown eyes shone.

Cassie knew Maggie had been wanting to go to this conference for years, but the church only slotted space for one participant. That spot always went to Roberta, who ran the women's group at the church. Maggie was a leader, but not the head.

"That's great news!" Cassie hugged her sister-in-law again. "When do you go?"

Maggie's eyes shifted toward Rick, who was in his own conversation with Daniel. She nudged his arm, and he turned back to the two women.

"So, can you do it?" Rick raised his eyebrows at Cassie.

"Do what?"

"I haven't asked her yet." Maggie elbowed him again.

"Oh. Maggie's going to the women's conference thingy tonight and has to pack today. Can you take her place at my open house this afternoon?" Rick was a real estate agent, and Maggie worked part-time for him when she wasn't working for Cassie in her Olde Crow Primitives country store.

"Oh, um..." Cassie hesitated. She was supposed to go birdwatching with the Banford Birding Club this afternoon. Those outings were the highlights of her month. She loved hanging out with her birding friends, especially Anna. They'd grown close over the last few months, and she didn't want to disappoint her. And she really wanted to go birdwatching.

"Do you two have plans for this afternoon?" Rick glanced back and forth between Cassie and Daniel.

She wished he wouldn't do that. Rick knew they were only friends. "No." Cassie shook her head. "But I'm supposed to go birding with Anna and the club."

"Pfft." Rick waved his hand. "You can help me then?"

"Play nice, Rick," Maggie chided her husband. He liked to tease Cassie about what he considered to be her strange hobby.

"Just kidding." He winked at Cassie. "But seriously, Sis. I know it's short notice, but it would really help me out. I need someone to sign people in while I show others the house."

Cassie chewed her lip and turned to Maggie. Her sister-in-law's face drooped like a lost puppy as she waited for Cassie's reply. As much as she loved birds, Maggie was much more important. "Of course I can help."

"Thank you!" Maggie's eyes sparkled again.

"But you owe me, Rick."

"I'll get you a cookie." He laughed and pointed to the baked goods table at the church café. "After you finish open house duty."

"Gee. Thanks." Cassie shot him a joking sneer and turned to Maggie. "How long will you be gone for?"

"It's only for two nights. I'll be back Tuesday evening."

"That sounds like—" Cassie's shoulders slumped as she realized what it meant. "Oh no! What about dinner tomorrow? You'll miss it!"

Thanksgiving Monday was Cassie's favourite day of the year. Gathering with the family for turkey dinner was a big event. For years, Grams held the festivities at her home, but after she retired and moved to a seniors' manor three years ago, Rick and Maggie began hosting the dinner.

At first it was difficult to change locations. Even though Cassie's mother had passed away ten years ago when Cassie was only eighteen, the memories of her still remained in Grams's old home. She'd adjusted to the change, but she couldn't imagine celebrating without her sister-in-law present.

"I know." Maggie grimaced. "I'm sorry. But I can't pass up this opportunity."

"Of course not." Cassie groaned. "Why do they have to have the conference on Thanksgiving weekend?"

"Tradition, I guess. Besides, most participants know way ahead of time and schedule their dinners on Sunday before they leave." Maggie frowned. "I'm really sorry I'm going to miss dinner."

"It's okay. I'm the one who's sorry." Cassie rubbed Maggie's arm. "I didn't mean to make you feel guilty."

"That's fine. I already—"

"There you are!" A short man in his thirties barged into the group and patted Rick on the shoulder. His bangs fell into his eyes as he peered at Cassie over the top of his thick-rimmed glasses and gave her a seductive smile. "Hey, Cassie."

Cassie refrained from wrinkling her nose by taking a sip of tea. After she swallowed, she forced out, "Hi, Wesley."

He pushed his way past Rick to the center of the social circle and faced Cassie. Daniel moved closer at the same time.

"I hear you're hanging out at my mom's house today." Wesley winked at her.

Cassie stepped back and glanced at Maggie and then Rick—both of whom avoided her gaze at the moment.

"I'm helping out my brother. I didn't know it was her house."

"Maybe we could grab a coffee afterward. You can let me know how it went." Wesley reached out and grabbed Cassie's hand. She tried to pull it away, but he gripped tightly.

"No, thank you." She yanked her hand again, this time escaping his grasp.

"How about dinner instead? It'd be great to spend time with you."

"Again, no, thank you." She leaned against Daniel and put her hand on his chest. "Have you met Daniel?"

Wesley squinted as he studied the man beside Cassie. "Yes."

"Hi, Wesley." Daniel held out his hand, but Wesley didn't accept the handshake.

Instead, he looked directly at Cassie again. "I'll see you later. At the house." He brushed against her shoulder as he strode past.

Maggie giggled.

"Seriously?" Cassie groaned and dropped her hand from Daniel's very strong chest. "Why didn't you tell me it was Wesley Clarkson's mother's house?"

"And spoil the surprise?" Rick grinned.

"And how did he know I was going to do it, when I only agreed a few seconds ago?"

Rick looked at the ceiling and whistled.

Daniel still stood close, his scent of leather and coffee stirring her senses. Cassie tried not to notice his biceps bulging underneath his tight sweater.

"Since when has Wesley returned his sights to you?"

"Since his latest internet girlfriend broke up with him." Cassie sighed. "At least I had a break for a little while."

Rick snickered.

"Be nice." Maggie leaned into Rick. "He's your friend, remember?"

"I'm not laughing at him. I'm laughing at my sister."

Cassie rolled her eyes. "To set the record straight, I'm doing this open house for Maggie, not for you."

"And I love you for it!" Maggie kissed Cassie on the forehead. "I'm going to go grab the girls so we can get home and I can get packing!"

"Okay." Cassie gave her a squeeze. "Have a great time."

"And I better find Grams and let her know the change of plans for tomorrow." Rick waved and headed off after his wife.

Daniel shifted to face Cassie directly. It felt like he stared straight into her soul. How did he do that?

He rubbed his chin. "You're sure I won't be intruding at the dinner?"

"Of course not! We're all glad you're coming." Cassie tilted her head and wrapped a curl around her finger. "Besides, Thanksgiving isn't meant to be spent alone."

Daniel's parents were on a cruise he bought for them as an anniversary gift, so he had no other dinner to attend this Thanksgiving weekend. As a famous landscape and celebrity photographer—

and now bookshop owner—he liked to share his wealth with those he loved.

She probably would've invited him to the Thanksgiving dinner anyway but was glad to use the cruise as an excuse. It helped keep things at the friendship level instead of implying anything more. The thankful leaves flashed through her mind.

Although he'd been attending church with her lately, Cassie had yet to see evidence of Daniel having a relationship with God. And even if he ever did, she still wouldn't jump into anything until he showed he had solid roots as a Christian.

She'd learned that lesson over four years ago when her former relationship went sour. Her old boyfriend had decided to share himself with other women on numerous occasions, including a month before their wedding.

Not that dating a Christian necessarily always prevented those types of things from happening, but since renewing her own faith after the breakup, she knew sharing her beliefs with her mate was the most important thing.

"What are you thinking about?" Daniel gently lifted her chin.

Cassie felt the heat rise to her cheeks from his touch. "Sorry. I spaced out for a sec. Hey—thanks for having my back with Wesley."

He smiled. "For the record, I'll always have

your back."

Heart fluttering, she silently urged God to hurry with drawing Daniel to Him.

"There you are!" Lexy bounced up to the non-couple. Her long hair was pulled back into a ponytail that bounced along with her. Striped leggings peeked out from underneath her long sweater. "I saw you chatting with Wesley. Did you agree to go out with him yet?"

"Oh, please."

Lexy giggled. "He's quite the catch, you know. His software company sold another app last week."

"Then why don't you date him?" Cassie winked.

"Nah. He has his heart set on you."

Daniel laughed and grabbed the empty cup from Cassie's hand. "Refill?"

"Sure! Thanks."

"Anything for you, Lexy?"

"I'm good. Thanks!" She held up her coffee cup as Daniel stepped away.

Lexy nudged Cassie's arm. "And Wesley's not the only one with his heart set on you."

"Stop." Cassie felt her cheeks warm again.

"You know it's true."

"And you know I can't."

"He's in church again..."

"I know." Cassie's eyes were drawn to the muscular figure walking toward the café. Her heart pounded in her chest. "I know."

Chapter 2

Cassie gasped as Rick drove down the long driveway to the Clarkson estate. Huge maples with fiery red and orange leaves lined both sides. At the end of the lane, a majestic stone home stood proudly, as if it earned a sense of regality by being there over a hundred and fifty years. The autumn sun reflected off the sparkling water of the Rideau Canal in the background, and a flock of geese flew overhead.

"Wow!" was all Cassie managed to say as Rick parked the car.

"Pretty nice, eh?" Rick grabbed his real estate folder from the back seat.

"Wesley grew up here?" Her mouth hung open after she spoke. She'd never been to Wesley's mother's home, even though Norma was friends with Grams.

"Yup. Want to change your mind about dating him?"

Cassie clamped her jaw shut. "Absolutely not." She glanced down the driveway from where they came. "When is he supposed to show up?"

Rick walked around the abundant flower gardens and up the flagstone walkway. "He's not coming. I told him it's better for business if the owner's family isn't around during the open house."

Cassie let out a sigh of relief. "Thank you."

"It wasn't only for you. It really wouldn't be good for him to harass potential buyers." Rick popped open the lockbox, grabbed the key, and let himself in the front door.

Stepping in after him, Cassie gasped again. The home was absolutely stunning. It still wore the original wide wood trim and wainscoting, all updated and painted a soft country grey. The tall windows and deep windowsills let in a lot of natural light, highlighting the polished hardwood floors and the high tin ceilings.

Following Rick through to the kitchen, she admired the mix of modern conveniences and colonial-style cupboards. He spread some house information sheets across the granite counters.

"I'm going to set you up at a small table by the front door. Your job is to welcome people, take down their names and addresses, and verify it against photo identification."

"I have done this for you before, you know."

"Sorry. It's been a while, so I wanted to refresh you." Rick straightened a pile of business cards.

"Are you nervous about this sale?"

"A little. I want to make sure Norma gets the price she deserves. And Wesley is putting on some pressure."

Cassie giggled. "Yes, he's good at that!"

"Plus there's a nice commission in it, and I'd love to surprise Maggie with a trip to Ireland for her birthday. If it comes through in time."

"Wow!" Cassie raised her eyebrows.

"But don't tell."

"Secret's safe with me." She winked. "I'll start setting up."

A lot of Norma's belongings had already been packed up and moved, leaving the place sparsely furnished, but Cassie managed to find a small folding table leaning beside the back door to use. As she looked through the window at the backyard, she gasped again at the unending beauty of the picturesque estate.

A garden-lined path led to a screened-in gazebo on a hill, overlooking the river far below. A boat bobbed at the dock. More trees in their fall splendour surrounded the backyard and filled the forest to the east. An old split rail fence guarded the property line to the west. It was stunning—

except for the numerous refilled holes in the yard.

"What were the holes from?" Cassie asked as she grabbed a kitchen chair.

Rick looked up from a folder. "Norma wanted to give a few small trees and shrubs to her neighbour before she moved. The gardener dug them up."

"She has her own gardener?"

"And housekeeper. And private nurse." Rick grinned. "Wesley looking like a better prospect yet?"

"Ugh. No!" Cassie rolled her eyes and carried the table and chair to the front entry.

Rick chuckled and resumed studying his notes.

Cassie set up the table and tucked the chair under the side. Back in the kitchen, she rummaged through some of the drawers, looking for a tablecloth, but Norma seemed to have had those packed already. The bare surface would have to do.

Rick handed her the sign-in form and a couple of pens marked with "Rick Bridgestone—Sales Representative" on the side. She dropped one into her purse with a grin and set the other on the table.

Cassie watched Rick wander the house to give everything a last check over and turn on all the lights. It was a realtor trick, making the house brighter and more appealing. She followed him room to room, trying to keep her mouth from hanging open as she admired the elegant bedrooms, each equipped with its own fireplace.

"Check this out!" Rick entered a room lined with bookcases, still half full of books. A large desk sat in the middle, a few stacks of papers in the corners.

"Oh!" Cassie gasped. "Her own library!"

"And..." Rick pulled on one of the bookcase shelves, and the whole thing swung out like a door. A small room appeared behind it, with more bookshelves and another desk.

Cassie clasped her hand over her mouth.

"*Now* do you want Wesley's number?" Rick snickered.

Cassie gave his arm a playful swat as she stepped into the hidden room. It was definitely the house of her dreams. "Norma's selling the house, remember? Wesley's not getting it."

"But if he was?"

She ignored his taunting and grabbed her phone from her back pocket, stealing a glance at the time. The open house was to start in five minutes. "I'd better get downstairs."

Sure enough, Cassie arrived at her post just in time to start receiving people coming in for the open house.

The first couple through had two teenage daughters in tow, who were seemingly more interested in their phones than the home. Cassie shook her head. Clearly, they didn't deserve to live in this grand home. The parents must have agreed because after a swift walk-through, they returned to their mustang and retreated down the driveway.

The next couple to sign in said they were moving out to the country from Ottawa. They took their time touring the house and were still upstairs when a gentleman with a short crew cut appeared at the doorway.

"Is this where I sign in?" He leaned against the doorframe, his hands shoved deep into the pockets of his cargo pants.

"Yes, it is!" Cassie greeted him and passed him the sheet and a pen. As he leaned forward, a set of military dog tags fell out of his shirt and swung toward the table. He quickly tucked them back behind his shirt neckline.

"You're in the military?"

"Yes." He slid the sheet across the table to her and pulled out his wallet.

"Army?"

He handed her his driver's licence. "Yes."

She looked over the identification and handed it back. Harlan Waller. Clearly Harlan wasn't a conversationalist. "Thank you."

Cassie was about to check off the identification box on the form when another man entered the door and walked past the desk. "Excuse me! You need to sign in, please."

The man continued on to the kitchen.

"Sir?" Cassie jumped up from her chair. "I need you to sign in."

"I just want a quick look around." He kept walking.

"I'm sorry, I still need you to—"

"Hey!" Harlan went after the man and grabbed his shoulder. "The lady asked you to sign in."

The man whipped around with a sneer on his face, scraggly hair covering his forehead and ears. Short and thin, he quickly relented after studying the muscular military man in front of him. "Yup. Sorry."

Harlan walked into the next room before Cassie had a chance to thank him. The other man tossed his licence on the table toward Cassie, making no move to fill out the sheet on his own.

Cassie inwardly sighed as she grabbed the identification and filled out the form for Mr. Jarvis Vinn. She held out the licence to him after she finished. "Here you go."

Jarvis Vinn merely snatched it from her hand, grumbled, and headed straight up the stairs to the second floor.

Cassie let out a slow breath. Who knew signing people into an open house could be so eventful? She looked forward to getting home and curling up with a good mystery book and her faithful cat and companion, Pumpkin. Thankfully, the next dozen or so people entered without a kerfuffle.

Things slowed down into the second hour, and Cassie found time to stand and stretch her legs. A few people still lingered. One couple was on their third walk-through of the house, while another had been chewing Rick's ear off with questions for the last twenty minutes.

Cassie smiled at her brother. He was in his element. Rick had spent years working near Toronto at a car dealership. Eventually, after he met and married Maggie, he tired of trying to convince city folk to trust him—a fallout from the nature of car sales. Rick and Maggie had decided to move back to his hometown of Banford, where he got a job in real estate. Selling homes was a whole new venture for Rick, and it was nice to work with people who valued his opinions. He instantly fell in love with the job and became one of the most trusted real estate salesmen in the county.

A bird chirped from her back pocket, signalling a text had come in. It was Anna.

Guess what we saw? Anna added a few bird emojis after her sentence.

What?

A northern parula! It's my first one!

Cassie groaned. Even though the bird was common, she had never seen a northern parula. She'd been wanting to add that bird to her life list for quite some time. And here she was at this open house instead of birding with the group. *Are you sure? It's October...*

Bill said it's a late fall straggler. Anna answered back.

Cassie's shoulders slumped. Bill was an expert birder and one of the most experienced in the Banford Bird Club. If he said it was a parula, there was no denying it. She forced herself to type, *That's great!*

"What's wrong, Sis?" Rick approached Cassie as the couple he had been speaking with stepped outside.

"Anna saw a parula." She shoved her phone in her back pocket.

"A what-a-what?"

"A bird. A good bird."

Rick frowned. "Oh. Sorry."

"It's okay. Maybe I can catch it later." She was certainly going to try.

"See them?" As he pointed through the window at the couple who had just left, Rick's frown suddenly turned into a smile that stretched from ear to ear. "They're going to put in an offer."

"That's great news!"

He glanced at his watch. "We're about done here. I'll see if the other couple has any questions, and we can lock up the house." He headed upstairs to find them.

Cassie brought the sign-in sheets to the kitchen and placed them on the countertop next to Rick's other documents. Then she took down the foldable table and returned the chair to the breakfast area.

As she tucked it under the table, the cellar door at the far end of the kitchen swung wide open. She jumped.

"Sorry. Did I startle you?" Harlan the military man appeared in the dark doorway.

"No. I didn't realize you were still here." Nor did Rick, she was sure. Where had Harlan been the whole time? In the cellar? Remembering his lack of conversation from earlier, he surely wasn't going to volunteer the information. "What were you doing down there?"

"Checking the foundation. They often need to be redone in old stone homes like this."

"Oh?"

"Canadian winters are harsh. But don't worry—this one's fine."

Cassie nodded. "Are you interested in the house, then?"

Harlan turned to look at her.

"Rick, the realtor, is upstairs. I can get him if you have any questions," she added.

"No, no. That's fine." Harlan headed toward the front door. "I'll think about it and get back to him if I'm interested."

Cassie grabbed a business card from the

counter and chased after Harlan. "Here!"

Already out the door, he leaned back in, took it from her hand, and shoved it in his pocket. "Thanks."

"Thanks for helping me with the other man earlier!" Cassie called after him.

Harlan merely lifted a hand in the air to wave without turning back to her. Cassie watched as he walked to his truck, hopped in, and backed out of the long driveway with impressive accuracy.

She stepped back into the house and closed the front door. Was he really checking out the foundation? Had he been in the cellar the whole time? It seemed so strange to her.

She crossed the kitchen to the open cellar door. As new and wonderful as the house was, a cold musty smell danced around her nostrils. She reached out above the stairs and pulled the string, turning the light on.

A narrow, wooden staircase with treads and no risers loomed beneath her. At the bottom, she could make out a rocky floor. She ignored the cobwebs overhead as she placed a foot on the creaky staircase. Slowly making her way down, she wrinkled her nose as the musty smell intensified.

Finally, Cassie stepped off the last tread. The coldness of the floor seeped through the soles of her flipflops, and she shivered. She pulled another light string, which immediately brightened the old space.

A furnace hung from the ceiling, suspended by metal straps. Old pallets sat on a gravelled area, and rubber totes were stacked on the pallets. To her right, the thick, stone wall glistened with moisture, and she didn't dare go near, fearful of the spiders that were sure to be lurking between the cracks of the old damp rocks.

Other than that, nothing seemed to jump out at her as suspicious. It was a large space, but there wasn't much down here. A couple of old doors leaned against the far wall, and an old wooden barrel sat in the corner.

Maybe Harlan really had been checking out the foundation.

She returned to the base of the stairs and turned out the light. As she put her foot on the first tread, the other light went out.

Above her, the door slammed shut, leaving her in total darkness.

With the spiders.

Chapter 3

"And then Cassie screamed so loud I thought the neighbours would come running!" Rick slapped his knee in laughter. "I was going to hold the cellar door shut so she'd think she was locked in, but I was laughing too hard."

"Yeah, it was hilarious." Cassie rolled her eyes. The only thing worse than Rick's practical jokes was falling for them. She turned to Grams. "Can you please pass the gravy?"

Grams reached past Daniel's plate to hand the boat to Cassie, pinching her lips together but failing to hide the smile.

"Were you scared, Aunt Cassie?" Lily asked with wide eyes.

"It just caught me off guard." She wiggled her fingers at Lily and her older sister, Olivia. "And there were spiders!"

"Ew!" the girls squealed and joined in the laughter.

The Bridgestone family and Daniel gathered around the spread of hearty food, celebrating Thanksgiving. A red tablecloth covered the table, and Maggie had made a centerpiece from a small pumpkin, red and orange leaves, and an orange candle. Surrounding the centerpiece were plates of turkey, honey-glazed ham, steaming mashed potatoes, green beans, gravy, and cranberries. All Cassie's Thanksgiving favourites.

There was something special about holiday dinners. Even though the Bridgestones gathered two or three times a month at Rick and Maggie's home for dinner, and usually once a month at Cassie's dad's place in the next town, Thanksgiving, Christmas, and Easter were still extra-special get-togethers. Maybe it was because of the spiritual significance of the holidays. Or perhaps it was simply because Cassie was sentimental.

"Did you have a good open house at Norma's yesterday?" Grams added some more ham to her plate.

"Yes. It was quite busy, actually." Rick scooped another forkful of mashed potatoes into his mouth.

"I'm not surprised. It's one of the nicest estates in the area."

Rick swallowed. "We already had an offer come in last night. Norma countered back this morning. We're just waiting to hear if they'll accept."

"I'm so happy for her." Grams put her fork down and clapped her hands together. "She was worried it would take a while to sell."

"Where is she moving to?" Daniel asked.

"She's already moved." Grams rubbed her hand across the tablecloth in front of her to smooth out a wrinkle. "She rented an apartment in the same manor I'm in at the Hudson Retirement Villa at the edge of town."

Cassie pried open a roll with her fingers. "What about all her stuff?" Even though the house had been mostly cleared out, she thought of all the remaining furniture and boxes at the estate.

"Most of her necessities are already taken care of." Grams used her fork to push around the green beans on her plate. "She just has to go through what's left at the house and decide what to do with it."

Rick's phone buzzed, and he pulled it out of his pocket. "Ha! She'd better decide soon because the house is sold!" His face lit up like a sparkler on Canada Day.

"That's great news!" Grams wiped her mouth with her napkin. "And a hefty commission for you, too, I bet!"

Rick smiled again. Cassie knew he was thinking

about the surprise trip to Ireland he'd planned for Maggie.

"Good job, Daddy!" Olivia patted her dad on the shoulder.

Daniel snickered and leaned over to Cassie. "She's so cute!"

"They both are," Cassie whispered back.

He stared deeply into her eyes. "They take after their aunt."

Cassie prayed her cheeks weren't as red as the cranberries on her plate. She looked at her food to avoid his gaze.

This was Daniel's first holiday dinner with the Bridgestone family, and it wasn't lost on Cassie how well he fit in. She felt his hand on her knee as he gave it a quick squeeze and let go again. Chills ran up her spine.

She took a deep breath to try to quell the tender feelings rising up within her. She had to resist. As the Bible said, she could not be unequally yoked to an unbeliever. Not again.

She caught Grams staring at her. She merely smiled and continued to dig into the food on her plate. Once again, Grams's words of wisdom ran through Cassie's mind. "Find someone who loves God more than you, and you more than himself."

"Thank you so much for allowing me to partake in your family dinner." Daniel interrupted Cassie's thoughts.

Rick chuckled. "Did you just say 'partake'?"

Cassie giggled too.

"What? Is that too much of an elite word for you simple country folk?" Daniel chided back.

"More like too much of an ancient word." Rick engaged in the banter. "What are you, seventy?"

"Hey!" Grams added. "I don't use that word, and I'm seventy-eight." After the laughter stopped, she turned to Daniel and patted his hand. "And you're welcome here anytime!"

"Thank you." Daniel turned to Cassie. "I hope to come here more often."

"When do we partake in dessert?" Olivia piped up.

Everyone laughed, and Cassie was grateful she didn't have to respond to Daniel's comment. Over the past couple months, he'd been understanding about the fact she only wanted a friendship. But lately he'd seemed to be pushing and hinting at something more again. As much as she didn't want to, she'd have to talk with him about it.

After dinner, Cassie and Grams cleared the table. Daniel offered to help, but Cassie insisted he stay seated. He chatted with Rick as the dishes were removed, the extra food put into containers, and the dishwasher started. She'd take him up on his offer after dessert, when the men could wash the pots and pans.

The girls squealed with delight as Grams

placed her old-fashioned apple pie on the table. It was everyone's favourite, including Cassie's. There was a special ingredient in it that Cassie had yet to figure out. Grams promised to give her the recipe—one day.

Beside the apple pie, Grams placed a pumpkin pie and a bowl of whipped cream. It wasn't only the little girls who licked their lips.

One hour, and seven full and satisfied stomachs later, Cassie poured herself a decaf Earl Grey and stepped out onto the back porch with Daniel. They sat side by side on the wooden porch swing and gently rocked as they looked out over the grassy meadow past Rick and Maggie's backyard. The setting sun cast hues of pink and purple across the sky. A swath of yellow-leaved poplars lined one side of the field, with towering oaks and evergreens on the other.

Cassie pulled her cardigan tighter around her as the autumn breeze blew through the backyard, bringing a cascade of crisp leaves with it.

"Are you cold?" Daniel put his arm around her and drew her close.

She pulled her knees to her chest and took a deep breath as she felt the muscles in his arm against her shoulders. He smelled like leather and old books. No, he smelled like… home.

Cassie closed her eyes and soaked in the comfort that was Daniel for another moment before she dropped her legs down, forced herself to shimmy forward, and made him release his grasp.

"Daniel…"

"What's wrong?"

She grasped her mug between the sweater sleeves she'd pulled over her hands. "I thought we were just friends."

Daniel instantly sat straighter and stopped rocking the swing. "We are."

"Are you sure?"

"Of course, I'm sure. Why?"

"I don't know." Cassie sighed. "Lately it feels like you think there might be something… more."

He turned to face her and put his finger under her chin, lifting it gently until she looked him in the eyes. "Isn't there?"

"You know I can't—"

He held his hand under her chin, not allowing her to look away. "Look me in the eyes and tell me I'm just your friend."

Cassie felt tears well up. "You're just my friend." She swallowed the lump in her throat.

He pulled away. "I don't believe you."

"You know how I feel about dating someone who doesn't share the same beliefs as I do."

"I've been going to church with you every Sunday."

"We've had this discussion before." She stared

at the deck boards. "Being a Christian means more than going to church. It's a relationship with God. It's living for Him, and putting Him first in everything."

"I believe in God, Cassie."

"Believing and following are two different things."

Daniel stared at his coffee cup as he swished the bit of remaining liquid around in the bottom. "I'm going to get a refill. Do you want one?" He pointed at her tea.

"No, thank you. I'm good."

He stood and went back into the house, leaving Cassie to rock by herself on the porch swing.

"Oh, God…" She raised her head to the darkening sky and spoke in a whisper. "Am I doing the right thing? I care so deeply for him…" She lowered her head. "But I want to honour You above all else. I need to keep You first. I won't pursue anything with Daniel unless he loves You wholeheartedly." She sniffed. "So, if that's not going to happen, please take these feelings away. Please stop my heart from yearning for him. It's too difficult."

Cassie shook her head and pulled her legs onto the porch swing, crossing them in front of her. She grasped her mug and stared out at the beautiful sunset. Her mind quieted. Her heart beat softly. And then the still, small voice she'd come to know spoke clearly to her heart.

"Wait, my child."

She was thrilled when she heard the voice of her Maker. "What do you mean, God?" Cassie whispered. "Does this mean Daniel will come around?"

"Wait."

"How long?"

"Wait."

Cassie sighed. She thought of her favourite Bible passage in Proverbs. It reminded her to trust in the Lord. To not try to figure it out on her own, but to keep looking to Him and let Him direct her paths.

She would wait.

Chapter 4

Lexy eyed Cassie over the top of the teacup she held to her lips. "So...."

"So... what?" Cassie pinched a small chunk off her pumpkin spice muffin and popped it into her mouth.

The girls sat together around a cute café table in The Tea Garden, their regular Tuesday morning meeting spot. Usually decorated with flowery Victorian décor, the proprietor had added a few fall touches. The antique vases on the tables held a fresh-cut mixture of orange and yellow mums. The portraits on the wall had been changed to a variety of Thomas Kinkade's fall paintings, and the pastry display window had been decorated with an orange-and-red leaf garland. The only thing missing was Maggie's company. She usually joined them but was still away at the conference.

"How was Thanksgiving dinner? With *Daniel*?"

"It was fine." Cassie pinched another piece off of her muffin.

"Just fine?"

"Mm-hmm."

"Spill it!"

Cassie sighed. "Okay, it was more than fine. It was wonderful. He was sweet, kind, and as charming as usual. After dinner we took our tea and coffee to the back deck and sat on the porch swing, watching the sunset. Better?"

Lexy hunched her shoulders and smiled. "Sounds wonderful!"

"And then I reminded him we're only friends, and he went back inside, leaving me on the porch alone."

Lexy dropped her shoulders and raised an eyebrow. "Seriously?"

"Seriously."

"Why would you do that?"

"It was an overdue conversation."

Lexy batted the air with her hand. "You're no fun."

Cassie glanced at her phone sitting on the café table. "And I'm about to be less fun. I have to run."

"Really? Why so early?"

"I promised Rick I'd drop some paperwork off to Norma Clarkson before I open the store. He has an appointment this morning, and Maggie's not back yet to help out."

"Fine." Lexy sighed and shoved the last bit of doughnut into her mouth. "But I'm coming over soon. I want more details!"

The girls exchanged hugs and left the Tea Garden. Cassie hopped into her car and headed out of Banford to the beautiful river estate, where Rick had told her Norma would be for the day. The house sale had a quick closing date, so Norma had even less time than originally planned to pack and remove the rest of her belongings.

Rick had promised Cassie that Wesley wouldn't be around this morning. He had plans to drop his mother off and head into the city for some errands. She hoped he'd been telling the truth. The last thing she wanted this morning was a surprise encounter with Wesley.

Cassie steered her SUV along the winding road following the Rideau River. It was especially beautiful this time of year, with the huge maples hanging over the water and the road, dispersing their leaves into a carpet of red, orange, and yellow.

She smiled at the autumn displays in front of people's houses. Big pumpkins, straw bales, scarecrows, and chrysanthemum plants greeted her at every turn. A murmuration of starlings twirled above a hayfield, and if she'd had more time, she would've stopped to enjoy their dance. It was one of her favourite bird displays.

She thought of the northern parula the bird club had seen on Sunday. She still hadn't had a chance to get out there and see if it was still around. Hopefully it would linger for another day or two.

Her destination was around the next bend. She pulled into the long driveway. Norma's estate still took her breath away, like she was seeing it again for the first time.

Cassie parked her SUV and grabbed the manila envelope from the passenger seat. She inhaled the fall air and smiled at the cardinal picking seeds from a birdfeeder hanging from the low-lying branch of a hundred-year-old maple.

The gravel crunched beneath her feet as she crossed the driveway toward the flagstone walkway. She couldn't imagine living in a place so grand and walking here every day. Whoever bought this home would be getting a taste of Heaven.

She started up the stone steps.

Boom!

Cassie felt herself being thrown backward as a wall of dust enveloped her.

She hit the ground with a thud, her ears ringing so loudly it pained her.

She lay there, trying to figure out what

happened. The thick cloud of dirt made it impossible to see.

Various spots on her arms and legs stung with fierceness, as if she'd been stabbed numerous times with a sharp dagger. Cassie tried to lift her head to look at herself, but the ringing in her ears grew louder, and her vision momentarily blurred.

When it cleared, a cloud of dust above her slowly dissipated, and bits of paper floated down from high in the sky.

What had happened?

As she tried to make sense of everything, a clear thought filled her mind.

Norma!

Cassie tried to sit up again, but her body hurt too much to cooperate. Instead, she continued to lie on the ground and forced herself to fight the pain in her arm and grab her phone from her back pocket, underneath her.

She managed to dial 911 and bring the phone to her ear. She winced as she noticed a piece of glass sticking out of the sweater on her forearm. It was surrounded by fresh blood stains.

A muffled voice came from the phone.

"Hello?" Cassie's voice was raspy and quiet. Was it even her voice? "Help," she whispered.

Her body was weary. She felt tired. Was that burnt toast she smelled?

She needed rest.

Cassie closed her eyes.

*****

What was that noise? Was she asleep? Dreaming?

Through the ringing in her ears, Cassie heard a roaring sound. And a siren. Why was it so hot? What was that smell?

The sirens wailed louder. Her ears hurt. The ground vibrated with a thumping noise. Someone was coming.

"Miss! Miss! Are you okay?"

Cassie opened her dry eyes. A man in a fireman's coat and hat leaned over her.

"Get the stretcher!" he yelled, hurting her ears even more. "Cassie, can you hear me?"

She tried to respond but moaned instead. More thumping. Another man appeared at her side. What was that roaring sound? And shouting? Lots of shouting.

Cassie felt herself being lifted onto the stretcher, and the two men carried her away. She managed to open her eyes a bit more and saw a mass of orange flames reaching to the sky.

No wonder she was hot.

The two firemen set her down in the cool grass and ran back toward the fire. Someone else dabbed her face with a wet cloth.

And then it hit her. The house! It was on fire! She sat up, fighting the resistance in her body. "Norma!" she cried. "There's a woman in the house!"

"What? Are you sure?" The person belonging to the voice appeared in front of her, a female paramedic.

"Yes! Please! Save her!"

The woman ran to the nearest fireman, who then shouted more orders to the other firefighters. Cassie watched as they attempted to enter the fiery inferno.

The woman returned and helped Cassie to sit up. She tended the puncture wound on Cassie's arm, two others on her legs, and scratches on her forehead. All the while, Cassie kept her eyes glued to the scene.

Firefighters sprayed water onto the massive orange blaze from all directions. Plumes of black smoke rose high into the sky. The far east wall of the stone home was still intact, along with a bit of the front corner, but the other walls had crumbled to the ground. The roof had already burned through.

"Miss Bridgestone. How are you?"

Cassie turned to see Officer Welby approaching. The tall, lanky policeman was assigned to visit Banford once a week at the Provincial Police satellite office, and for any other crimes needing attention. While he was here, Lexy was shifted from her job as a municipal office assistant to the loathsome job as Welby's personal secretary.

"I'm okay, I think." She brushed a curl out of her eyes and stood, surprised he cared. She wasn't his favourite Banford resident.

Officer Welby pulled a notepad from his pocket and flipped it open. "I need a statement. Can you tell me what happened?"

What did happen? Cassie wasn't exactly sure. She was here to bring paperwork to Norma. She approached the house and—

"An explosion!" It all came back to her. "I was thrown backward, and..." She thought a moment. "And then the firetrucks were here, and the firemen carried me to safety."

Officer Welby shifted his weight onto one foot. "Are you sure you're telling me everything?"

"Yes—I think so." Suddenly she wasn't so sure.

"Was anyone else on the premises?"

"Norma was in the house."

"Are you positive? Did you talk to her?"

"Well, no." Cassie furrowed her brows. Maybe Norma wasn't here. Maybe she was safe after all. "But I came here to meet her."

"No other cars in the driveway?"

"None that I can remember."

"All right." Officer Welby flipped the notebook

shut. "I might call you in for further questioning once you're feeling better."

Cassie nodded and took a seat on the rear of the ambulance, letting her sore legs dangle out of the back. She gave Grams a quick call and filled her in, assuring her over and over her injuries weren't serious. None of her cuts had required stitches, and the bump on her head was minimal, considering the circumstances. The paramedic had assured her she'd heal quickly.

After convincing Grams she didn't need to come to the scene, Grams agreed to go and open the shop for Cassie. She was going to take Maggie's later morning shift anyway.

The fire seemed to be under control now, albeit there wasn't much left to burn at this point. The firefighters still doused the rubble with water, but it appeared they were taking turns now instead of all tackling it at once.

A fireman with soot on his face walked toward Cassie. He stopped at a truck to remove his helmet, revealing shoulder-length locks soaked in sweat. He pulled off his thick firefighter coat and hung it on a bar protruding from the back of the truck.

Chest muscles bulged through his tight-fitting shirt, and his large biceps glistened from perspiration. A tattoo of a compass rose peeked out from under the edge of his sleeve.

Cassie gulped.

He stared at her as he approached, and she found she couldn't look away from his deep-green eyes.

"How are you feeling?" His voice was gruff but gentle.

"I'm better. Thank you." She studied his face. There was a familiarity about it. "Were you one of the men who brought me away from the house?"

He nodded. "Yes. And in the nick of time. See that pile of rubble over there?" He pointed to a heap of old stone where one of the walls had collapsed. "That's where you were lying when I found you."

Cassie's stomach flipped. This man had saved her life. "Thank you for helping me."

"Anytime, Cassie."

How did he know her name? "Do I know you?"

He laughed. "You don't recognize me? Not that I should be surprised. I'm Spencer Kingsley."

Spencer Kingsley? The scrawny, geeky kid who spent all his time in the library in high school?

"Um… your mouth is hanging open a bit." He chuckled.

Cassie clamped her jaw shut. "Uh, sorry. I—"

"It's okay. Are you sure you're feeling better?"

She nodded. "Have you been back in Banford long?" If she remembered correctly, he left town after graduating. Even though they didn't really talk in high school, with the small senior class of only fifty people, it was easy to know who everyone else was, and what their plans were after they finished grade twelve.

"A couple of years." He scratched at some of the soot on his face. "You can't take the country out of a Banford boy."

"Or girl." She grinned.

"Kingsley!" A firefighter yelled over from the truck.

"Gotta run. Nice seeing you!" He winked and gave her a thin smile that lit his eyes.

Cassie swallowed and gave a little wave. Wow. She'd have to tell Lexy about Mr. Spencer Kingsley. Perhaps there was hope for Lexy's love life, yet.

Spencer suddenly returned to Cassie, but the smile was long gone. In its place stood a concerned frown.

"What's wrong?" Cassie stood, ignoring the pain shooting through her thigh.

"The lady you mentioned…"

"Norma?"

"Yes. We've found her." He ran his hand through his hair. "I'm sorry, Cassie. She didn't make it."

Chapter 5

Cassie winced as she raised her arm to adjust a display of candles on a shelf in Olde Crow Primitives. After a long bath and a short sleep, Cassie had been restless and returned to work around two o'clock.

"Are you sure you're all right?" Grams came over and gently placed her arm on Cassie's back. "I can handle the shop if you want to go upstairs and get more rest."

"I'm fine. I'd rather keep busy."

"If you insist." Grams walked to the cash counter to ring up a customer's purchase of autumn mini lights decorated with leaves.

An orange-and-white bundle of fur bounded up to Cassie. "Meow?"

"Hi, Pumpkin!" Cassie picked up her oversized

tabby and cradled her. Pumpkin purred in response and flicked her tail through the air.

Being able to bring her cat to work was pure delight. Every morning when Cassie left her upstairs apartment for work, Pumpkin would eagerly bound down the stairs after her, follow her to the store, and jump into her cushioned bed behind the cash counter. The customers loved her too. There was something about a cat that added to the country feel in Olde Crow Primitives.

The century building stood on the corner of Main Street and First Street, near the only traffic light in Banford—not there for the intersection, but rather to stop drivers when the swing bridge opened to allow boat traffic through the town's lock system.

When Grams retired, she'd struck a deal with Cassie to hold over the mortgage so Cassie could buy the building at an affordable price. It housed three stores—Olde Crow Primitives, The Chocolate Shoppe, and The Book Nook in the back, run by Daniel. Cassie's apartment was on the second floor along with another apartment she rented out full-time to a sweet older lady. On the third floor, there were three apartments. One Daniel rented, and two others Cassie rented out on a weekly basis to vacationers. Banford attracted a lot of tourists during the summer and its special Christmas Festival.

Cassie nuzzled the cat's nose, put her down, and checked the display in the large front window. Wooden pumpkins, plaid pumpkins, and plastic pumpkins surrounded the wooden signs welcoming fall. A black lantern stuffed with deep-orange and dark-red silk flowers acted as the centerpiece, and gourds, black cat figures, and garlands of leaves and lights accented the display. She reached in to straighten a pyramid tower of apple-cider-scented candles and breathed in the fragrance of fall.

"Have a great day!" Grams called to the woman leaving through the front door.

Cassie turned to her grandmother. "How about you? Are you okay? Losing a friend can't be easy."

Grams sighed. "Norma was a good friend who will always hold a special place in my heart. I'll miss her dearly, but I can mourn in my own time. Right now, you need me here."

"Are you sure?" Cassie studied her grandmother's face.

"Positive."

For the next while, Cassie busied herself unpacking the latest shipment of fall candles. She filled the display and added a few candles to various shelves throughout the store.

Busy. She had to keep busy.

But despite her efforts, she couldn't get the fire out of her mind. The whole time she'd been on the ground, and later on the stretcher, poor Norma had been trapped inside the burning house. What had even caused the explosion? And why did it burn after?

Over and over, the scene played through her mind.

She did some dusting and rearranged the wooden and rustic items on two or three shelves. Grams handled most of the customers who came into the store, but Cassie also served a few herself.

Around four o'clock, she gave up trying to think of other things, so she ran across the street to Drummond's Bakery. Maybe doughnuts would help. It couldn't hurt to try.

Cassie returned with an apple fritter for herself and a Boston cream for Grams. They sat together behind the counter, enjoying their pastries and sipping tea.

"It keeps running through my mind, Grams." Cassie dusted some crumbs off her sweater.

"I know, dear. It will for a while." She patted Cassie's leg. "As it does, continue to bring it to God. He'll help you heal."

Cassie nodded and downed the rest of her tea. She tossed the paper cup in the garbage and returned to straightening the summer clearance rack she'd worked on before lunch.

"Cassie!" Daniel appeared through the back-door entrance leading to the hallway between their stores. "I just heard. Are you okay? Why didn't you call me?"

She gingerly hopped off her stool and met him in the middle of the store. "I'm fine." How many times would she have to say that today? And why *hadn't* she called him?

"You don't look fine!" He gently put her hair behind her ear and studied the scratches above her eye. He grabbed her hand and held it in his own.

Chills ran through Cassie's body, as they always did when he touched her. At least that part wasn't broken. "Really, I—"

"What about your head? You should be resting. You could have a concussion!"

She pulled her hand away. No one was going to let her off the hook. "I'll rest later if I don't feel well."

"If you're sure."

"I am." She looked over his shoulder toward the back wall. "Is anyone in your store?"

"A few customers. It doesn't matter. People browse for a long time. I had to make sure you were all right."

"Thanks."

"If there's anything I can do…" He grabbed her hand again.

Cassie smiled at him. He was so caring, so… loving. "I'll ask. Don't worry."

"Make sure you do." He gave her hand a squeeze before he let go.

Her knees weakened, and it wasn't from her injuries. She watched as he started back to his store and reprimanded herself for noticing how well his jeans fit.

Just friends. Wait. Cassie ran the words through her mind to remind herself.

"Cassie?" Grams called from the front of the store. "There's a gentleman here to see you."

Cassie peeked out from behind the display of lanterns. A strikingly handsome man in ripped jeans and a tight sweater waved at her. His long hair teased the top of his shoulders. Spencer. He cleaned up nicely.

"Who is *that*?"

She whirled around to see that Daniel hadn't returned to his store at all. He peered over her shoulder with narrowed eyes.

"Just a guy I went to school with. He was the firefighter who rescued me at the scene." Was her face red? It felt a bit warm.

"Hmmm." Daniel ran his hand through his hair.

"Hi, Spencer." Cassie stepped forward to greet him.

Daniel followed at her heels.

"Hi." His gruff voice suited his husky appearance. "I thought I'd stop in and see how you were doing."

"I'm fine, thank you." *Again.* Maybe she should make a recording.

"I'm Daniel." Daniel pushed by her and stuck his hand out to Spencer. "I'm Cassie's—"

"Friend." Cassie smiled at him. "And tenant. He runs The Book Nook at the back of the building and rents one of the apartments upstairs." She felt the warm air blowing out of Daniel's nostrils.

"Nice to meet you." Spencer shook hands. Cassie was sure the two men held their grips longer than was necessary.

"Thank you for saving Cassie."

"Of course." Spencer nodded.

"She's very important to me. I'd hate to have anything happen to her." Daniel glared at Spencer.

What was he doing? Cassie rolled her eyes. Men. "Daniel was just heading back to his store, isn't that right?"

He turned his sights on Cassie, saving a bit of his scowl for her. "I'll see you later." He tilted his head to the side and walked rather briskly to the back door.

Spencer leaned to his left to look past Cassie. "Seems like a nice guy..." He raised an eyebrow.

"Never mind about him. Thank you for coming to check on me." Cassie put a stray curl behind her ear. "How did you know I worked here?"

Spencer laughed. "It's Banford, remember? I asked at the firehouse if anyone knew how I could find you, and one of the guys mentioned you owned this building."

"Oh." She felt heat in her cheeks again. He'd specifically asked about her? "Any news as to what caused the explosion and the fire?"

"The fire marshal is at the scene now. He'll report his findings by the end of the day. The rubble is still pretty hot, though. It may take him a few days to find the source."

"That makes sense." Cassie nodded.

"Rowr?" Pumpkin appeared and rubbed herself against Spencer's leg.

"Well hello, kitty!" He bent down to scratch the top of the cat's head. "Can I pick her up?"

"Uh, sure." Really? Not the reaction she would have expected from this brawny man.

Spencer lifted Pumpkin and cradled her in his arms like a baby. "What's her name?"

"Pumpkin." Cassie raised her eyebrows. "Careful. She doesn't like to be held like that by strangers."

"I think she's fine." Spencer cooed at the cat, who lay back in his arms, enjoying the belly rubs. "Hey listen. I have a night shift tonight at the station. If you're not busy, why don't you come by around six thirty, and I'll let you know if the fire marshal found anything today."

"That would be great. Thank you!" Cassie stared at her over-comfortable cat.

Spencer set Pumpkin onto the floor.

"Good. I'll see you tonight then." He stood straight, winked, and smiled. His smile could be pretty charming too.

But it didn't hold a candle to Daniel's.

Chapter 6

Banford Fire Hall was situated on a quiet street past the south end of the village. Cassie turned her SUV into the driveway and pulled into a spot beside a green Dodge Challenger with black racing stripes. Two vans were also in the lot. She guessed the green muscle car to be Spencer's.

Cassie grabbed her phone and tossed the purse onto the passenger seat. There was no need to bring the whole thing inside with her, and she knew it would be safe in her unlocked car. It was Banford, after all.

She stepped out into the autumn breeze, shoved her phone in her back jeans pocket, and pulled her favourite fall cardigan tighter around her. A swirl of red leaves danced in the parking lot before blowing onto the grass. The sun had already set. She loved twilight in the fall.

"Hey! You made it!" Spencer stood in the open fire truck parking bay, his folded arms above his head, leaning on the overhead door.

Cassie ignored the way his biceps stretched the sleeves of his tight cotton shirt and entered the bay. "Hi."

"It's great to see you. You look pretty good for someone who survived an explosion." He dropped his arms, crossed them in front of his chest, and stood with his feet comfortably apart.

"I'm sure I'll feel it in the morning."

Spencer chuckled. "I bet! You're a lucky girl."

Cassie smiled and stared into his sparkling green eyes. She opened her mouth to speak but was at a complete loss for words. Awkward much?

"Come on back to the break room." He stretched out his arm to show the way. "We can chat in there."

"Sure," she squeaked out as she followed him into the small lounge-like area and picked a comfy couch to sit on.

Spencer grabbed a remote control from the coffee table and turned off the hockey game playing on the big-screen television. "Can I get you a tea?"

"No thanks. I had one before I came over here." She studied his expression. "How did you know I drank tea and not coffee?"

"Good guess." He smirked and sat on the sofa beside her.

Cassie moved a little closer to her end and scanned the room. "Is no one else working tonight?"

Spencer shook his head. "The chief is still here, chatting it up with the fire marshal. They're old buddies." He nodded his head toward an office door through the large lounge window. "But then it's only me until Rob gets in. He comes after his kids are in bed and he's spent a bit of time with his wife."

Cassie furrowed her brows. "There are only two of you working the night shift?"

"We're lucky to have enough volunteers to run night shifts at all."

"Volunteers? You're not paid?"

"Nope." Spencer shook his head. "The county fire stations are small and completely run by volunteers. The only one who gets paid is the chief."

Cassie couldn't believe what she was hearing. "So how do you... live? If you don't mind me asking."

"I have a regular job. I work construction up near Ottawa four days a week."

"And then you come here and volunteer overnight?"

"Two evenings during the week, and overnight

on my day off." He ran his fingers through his long hair.

"Wow. Okay." Lexy definitely had to meet this guy.

"It's no big deal, really. I don't have a family like most of the guys. They're the ones who really sacrifice."

Cassie grinned. Firefighters really were heroes.

"So, do you want to hear what the fire marshal found?" Spencer leaned into the couch and rested his arm across the top, his hand inches from her shoulder. His compass tattoo hugged the muscles in his bicep.

"Definitely!"

"Don't be too eager. You're not going to like it."

"Why? What do you mean?" Cassie drew her leg onto the couch in front of her.

Spencer reached out his hand and put it on her knee. "It was deliberate."

"Arson?" Cassie gasped and pulled her leg out of his reach.

"Not exactly. But close. The explosion was deliberate, and the fire happened as a result."

"How do you know?"

"The marshal found traces of explosive residue in the rubble near the cellar. That's where it was set. And they found pieces of the detonation cord used to ignite it."

"You mean the person who did it was there

when it happened? There was no timer?"

Spencer nodded.

Cassie rubbed her forehead. Had the person seen her when she neared the house? She was pretty sure no other cars had been in the driveway. "And the fire?"

"It originated in the kitchen, on the opposite side of the house from the explosion. He's still gathering evidence and there's more to go through, but it looks like the stove element was on and the impact of the blast caused something to land on it and catch fire. A sweater, or a dish towel maybe. From there, the fire ignited the wooden cupboards and then the trim."

"Poor Norma!" Cassie covered her face with her hands.

"It doesn't look like she suffered." Spencer inched forward and dropped his hand from the back of the couch onto Cassie's shoulder. "She was upstairs at the time. She must have been boiling water or something and went to the bedroom in the meantime. The medical examiner said she had quite the trauma to her skull, consistent with being knocked out by the impact of the explosion. She was already unconscious before the smoke or the fire reached her. She wouldn't have felt anything."

Cassie sniffed and wiped away a tear. She barely knew the woman, but being there while the tragedy happened changed everything.

"There's more." He gently rubbed her shoulder.

"Because the explosion caused a fire, and the fire killed Mrs. Clarkson, it's now become a murder investigation."

"What?" Cassie jumped to her feet and out of Spencer's grasp. "Who would want to kill Norma?"

"Officer Welby was here earlier, talking with the fire chief and the marshal."

"And?"

"They've taken her son into custody."

"*Wesley?*" Cassie shook her head. "Impossible! He wasn't even there!"

"They aren't sure he wasn't. And he has motive. Between the hefty house insurance policy on the estate, and the life insurance policy on his mother, Wesley stands to make a fortune."

"That doesn't make sense! If he wanted to kill her for money, wouldn't he wait until after the sale of the house? I know how much she sold it for. I doubt any insurance policy would touch that."

"I overheard Officer Welby say that it did. Because of the heritage factor on the house, the replacement cost was huge. The policy was worth far more than the sale."

Cassie sat again. "This is ridiculous. It's Wesley, for Pete's sake! He couldn't hurt a fly—annoy it to death maybe, but never hurt it."

"There's something else you should know."

"What?" Cassie huffed.

"They found traces of TNT in the trunk of Wesley's car."

"I don't believe it." Cassie shook her head. "There's no way he was involved."

Spencer shrugged. "I'm only the messenger. I don't even know the guy."

"This whole thing is getting more bizarre by the minute."

"I'm just glad we got there before you became part of the crime scene."

"Me too." Cassie smiled at Spencer and rose to her feet. "I should get going. Thank you for the information."

"Sure." He stood, led her to the door, and held it open for her. "I'll walk you to your car."

Spencer followed Cassie out to the fire truck bay and outside to her SUV. With only a few remnants of daylight left, the large overhead lights surrounding the parking lot had turned on and illuminated the area.

"I'm guessing that's your sporty ride?" She pointed at the green muscle car.

"Yeah." His voice seemed a tad gruffer than usual. "I fixed it up myself."

"Nice." Something above the dash caught Cassie's eye. A leather cross dangled from the rearview mirror. "Is that a cross?" Shoot. Why did she say that out loud?

"Yup. My niece gave it to me." He ran his fingers

through his hair, but it only parted and fell back around his face. "I taught her Sunday School class how to make necklaces one week."

What? Cassie's eyes opened wide. "*You* taught Sunday School?"

"Teach. Present tense." He grinned. "Every third Sunday."

"What church?"

"Rideau Baptist, up on the hill."

"I..." Cassie couldn't believe it. "You're a believer?"

"You say that like you know what it means, Cassie Bridgestone."

"I-I do. I am. Too... I mean." Why was she stuttering?

"Yes. I am. I turned to Christ after making some bad decisions when I lived in the city. My life hasn't been the same since."

Cassie grinned. God never ceased to amaze her by the people He reached.

"Where do you go to church?" Spencer leaned against his car, his tight jeans barely stretching over the muscles in his thighs.

"Northwood, at the edge of town."

"I've heard great things about Northwood. I'd like to try it sometime."

"That'd be nice." The words spewed out of Cassie's mouth before she knew what she was saying.

He crossed his arms in front of him again and tilted his head. His hair fell, brushing the top of his shoulder.

"Well, uh. I should get going." Cassie pulled out her phone and looked at the blank screen.

Spencer nodded at her phone. "Why don't we exchange numbers, and I can let you know if they find anything else at the crime scene?"

"Okay." Cassie swiped her screen and maneuvered to the contact page. She typed in his name and handed him the phone. He brushed her hand as he took it from her.

After a few quick thumb movements, he handed it back. "Here you go. And I sent myself a message from it, so I have your number."

Cassie slipped the phone back into her pocket. "Sounds good. Thanks for the info!" She waved and climbed into her SUV.

"Bye, Cassie." He said her name so deeply and gently.

He continued to lean against his car until she drove all the way out to the road and turned toward Banford.

Spencer was a Christian, Norma was murdered, and Wesley was in custody. Could this day get any weirder?

Chapter 7

"So, can you help?" Rick's voice was way too chipper for Cassie's foggy morning brain.

She held the phone to her ear and stretched out in her bed. Pain left over from yesterday's injuries darted through her muscles. "What? Say that again?"

"C'mon, Cass, wake up!"

She held out her phone to check the time. "It's only seven!"

"And you'll need to get up now, so you have time to go."

"Are you coming with me?"

Rick hesitated. "No. I have a house showing at nine."

"Seriously? You want me to help Wesley, and you're not even going with me?"

"Yeah. Sorry. The cops will be right outside the door, so you can call for help if he hits on you." Rick chuckled.

"Not funny."

"Please?" His tone turned serious again. "He's my friend, and you know as well as I do, he didn't murder his mom."

"And how can talking to him help?"

"Stop being stubborn. You've solved a murder case before. Why should this be any different?"

Cassie groaned. "Fine. I'll go. But I can't make any promises."

"Thanks, Sis! Gotta run."

Cassie tossed her phone on the nightstand and sat up in the bed. A furry mass landed on her wiggling toe. "Ouch! Pumpkin!"

The cat crouched in the mess of sheets, mischievously twitching her tail. Cassie straightened the bedding, being sure to pull a heavy quilt over her legs and feet. Then she darted her foot across the bed, keeping it under the covers.

Pumpkin jumped and landed on Cassie's foot, attacking it with her claws. Cassie quickly moved it to the other side, laughing as the cat chased it again. Pumpkin's extra fluff jiggled as she ran back and forth across the bed, wide-eyed, trying to catch her prey.

When she'd had enough, Pumpkin waddled

over to Cassie for some ear scratches. Cassie obliged.

Eventually, Cassie climbed out of bed. She flattened her tousled curls with her hand as she crossed the apartment to the living room window overlooking the Rideau River. The morning sun shimmered on the water's surface. A few fall leaves fell onto a boat, already waiting to get through the locks when they opened at nine. Next week, the lock system would be closed for the season, so despite the chilly air, a few eager boaters travelled through for their last tour of the year.

Cassie smiled as a few tree swallows darted from side to side in the air, catching their breakfast. She thought about the northern parula. She'd hoped to try to catch a glimpse of it this morning, but now that plan was ruined.

She scolded herself for thinking so selfishly. Even though Wesley annoyed her, Rick was right. He needed help. Perhaps there would be enough time after her visit to stop and see the bird.

After a quick shower, Cassie picked out a pair of jeans and a dark-orange shirt. It was one of her fall favourites because the sleeves were long and hung over part of her hands. She covered it with a stylish orange, red, and blue plaid shirt, and pulled on her brown knee-high boots. The soles were flat with thick treads, so if she had time to go birding, she could handle the trail terrain.

As she walked into the kitchen, Pumpkin gave a loud meow. She stood eagerly by her food dish, waiting for breakfast. Cassie filled it and opened the fridge to see what she could make for her own meal. The cat lay down to eat.

She checked the time. If she left right now, she could stop at Drummond's Bakery to get a doughnut. Not the healthiest meal, but if she had to stomach a visit with Wesley, she figured she deserved a pastry.

Thirty minutes and one powdered jelly doughnut later, Cassie pulled into the county police station. The Banford office was only a satellite location and didn't have jail facilities, so prisoners were transferred to the county station for holding.

She grabbed her purse from the passenger seat and glanced in the rearview mirror. There was powder on her chin. Should she leave it there? Maybe it would help ward Wesley off her. On the other hand, he might take it as an invitation to touch her face. She wiped it off.

The officer at reception buzzed Cassie through the foyer doors and led her to a back room where she could wait for Wesley. A table surrounded by three chairs stood in the center. Cassie opted for the side with one chair, to dissuade Wesley from sitting directly beside her.

Moments later, an officer escorted him into the room. His hands were in cuffs.

"Cassie! Thank you for coming." He reached his arms out, but she stayed seated.

"Hi, Wesley."

He sat opposite her and stretched his arms across the table. She sat back so he couldn't reach her.

"I knew you'd come to help." He winked.

She chose not to react. "Rick insisted I come. I'm not sure what I can do, though."

"I'm sure you'll figure something out. You're the smartest girl I know." Now he gave her a silly grin.

This wasn't going to be easy. "Why don't you tell me anything you think could be helpful?"

He leaned back into his chair with a sigh and pulled his cuffed hands into his lap. "I don't know what to say. I dropped Mom off, headed to the city, and..." His face paled. "Then I got a call."

Cassie inwardly groaned. She didn't like Wesley, but that shouldn't make her lose sight of the bigger picture. He'd lost his mother, and he was being blamed for it. Her heart softened a little, but she proceeded with caution.

"I'm sorry about your mother. I wish I could have done something to save her."

His eyes welled up with tears. "Thank you. I know you would've if you were able. I'm just glad you weren't killed too."

Cassie grabbed a tissue from her purse and handed it across the table to Wesley. He snivelled into it.

"Okay. Let's go over the facts." Cassie sat straighter. "Who else knew you were dropping your mom off at the house? Did anyone know she'd be there alone?"

Wesley shook his head. "I don't think so. It's possible, but I don't really know for sure."

"What about your errands in the city? What time did you plan on coming back?"

"I thought I'd be gone about three or four hours." Wesley put the snotty tissue onto the table. "I figure that would give Mom enough time to pack a few more boxes and I could load them into the car for her when I returned."

"You didn't have to work yesterday?"

Wesley shook his head. "Some of the errands were work related, but I'd planned on taking the rest of the day to help Mom. I was going to move out the remaining furniture after I dropped her off at home with the boxes." He sighed. "I guess I don't have to worry about any of that now."

Wesley was right. All their plans had changed in a moment. And now he was without a mother. "Where exactly did you go? Surely someone can prove you were in the city during the time of the explosion. What did you buy? Do you have receipts? Maybe you're on a camera somewhere."

He sighed. "That's what I told the cops, but they say it doesn't add up. First, I went to the coffee shop in Kemptville, and then I sat by the river to drink and eat before I headed to the city. I didn't feel like taking the busy highway, so I took the long way on the country backroads."

"Where there are no cameras."

"Exactly. And they said the gap of time between the coffee and my first stop in the city left me enough time to come back here and cause the explosion first."

Cassie wasn't sure what else to ask him. She thought about her favourite British mystery shows and the cozy mystery novels she read. What would the sleuth do?

Motive. Who had a motive for murdering Norma?

"I didn't do it. You know that, right?" Wesley stared at her with pleading eyes.

"I know. But it doesn't look good. There's a lot of money that stood to come your way from the insurance. Not to mention the TNT residue in your trunk."

"I don't know how to explain that. Someone must have planted it there." Wesley's shoulders slumped. "And as for the money, I don't need it. My software company is doing really well. Mom even planned to give me some of the house proceeds, but I refused. I told her to keep it for a holiday or something."

"Did anyone hear you tell her that?" Cassie asked, already sure the answer would be no.

Wesley shook his head.

"What about showing the police your bank account? Then they can see you didn't need the insurance money."

"Nope. I'm in the process of securing a big loan for a new international project. They think I wanted Mom's money to avoid interest."

"Okay. Then who else had it in for your mother? Did she have any enemies? Who else will gain from her, uh, passing?"

Wesley shrugged. "I don't know. I've been going over it in my head all night. It's not like I could sleep on the raggedy cot they gave me, anyhow."

"So, you have no idea at all?"

"No. Sorry."

Cassie sighed. This was going to be way harder than she thought. Maybe she should just let the police handle the investigation. Surely, they would see Wesley's innocence by talking to him and continue looking for other suspects.

But no, that wasn't true. Officer Welby liked to have a quick and clean case, and he was in charge of this investigation. Her past experiences had shown her he didn't worry about looking further into a case if he already had a reason to charge someone. If anyone was going to get Wesley out of this mess, it had to be her.

"What about when you were at the open house with Rick?" Wesley asked. "Did you see anyone suspicious lurking around?"

The open house. Of course! Cassie had forgotten all about it. It seemed so long ago. But as it jumped to the forefront of her mind, she remembered one specific military man lurking around in the cellar a long time. The cellar where the explosion happened. She wracked her brain to remember his name. Harlan? That sounded right.

And what about the man who didn't want to sign in? What was his story? Cassie pictured the sign-in sheet. Not only did it have a complete list of names of everyone who came to the open house, it had their identification and address information as well.

"You might be on to something, Wesley." Cassie stood. "I'll see what I can find out." She skirted around the table toward the door.

Wesley grabbed her hand as she walked by. "Thank you." The sorrow faded from his eyes, and an oversized smile appeared on his face. "You're so amazing, Cassie. When you get me out of here, I promise I'll make it up to you. I'll take you out for a wonderful dinner and—"

"No thanks necessary." She pulled her hand

back. "Like I said, I promised Rick I'd help." Although the way he looked her up and down made her want to leave him in jail.

"Come back and see me."

"If I have to," she muttered as the guard opened the door.

Cassie didn't like having anything to do with Wesley. The sooner she solved this case, the better. At least she now had a direction to follow.

She had to get the open house list from Rick.

Chapter 8

A squirrel skittered across the trail in front of Cassie, chattering to express its annoyance at her presence. She walked at a quick pace, anxious to get to the part of the forest where the Banford Bird Club members had seen the northern parula on Sunday. She had only about thirty minutes before she had to head back to Banford, giving her time to stop at Rick's office and get the open house sign-in list before she headed to Olde Crow Primitives and opened the store for the day.

The chances of seeing the parula were slim. As a late fall migrant, it wouldn't waste much time hanging around. It would want to move south quickly. Even so, Cassie couldn't pass up the opportunity to check. She'd been wanting to add the parula to her life list for years. It wasn't a rare bird or anything, but for some reason it had always eluded her.

Cassie slowed as she approached the section of forest where it had been spotted. A movement in the trees caught her eye, so Cassie stopped and lifted her binoculars. Just a chickadee.

She scanned the treetops. Parulas normally liked to hang out high in the canopy, but during migration they could be found lower, foraging for food. She walked slowly down the path, listening intently for the bird's buzzy trill and scanning the forest for movement. Five minutes passed. Then ten. Fifteen.

Cassie sighed. She needed to head back. She'd have to make more time this week to return.

Moments later, she pulled her SUV into the tiny parking lot beside Rick's real estate office. As she walked in the door, Maggie looked up from behind a filing cabinet.

"Cassie!" She came over to give her a hug.

"Hey, Mags. How was the conference?"

"It was wonderful! I'll tell you all about it later." She stood back and looked at Cassie with wide eyes. "First I want to hear about your incident. I'm so glad you're all right."

"Thanks. It was a little crazy."

"I was only gone for two nights. I can't believe everything that happened." Maggie shook her head and clucked her tongue. "Thank you for helping Wesley. This must be so hard for him."

"Yeah, he's pretty shaken up."

"Any leads yet?"

"Actually, that's why I'm here." Cassie pointed at the reception desk. "Can I get a copy of the sign-in sheet from the open house? There's a few people I want to check out."

"Sure." Maggie plucked a sheet out of a stack of papers in a letter tray, brought it to the photocopier, and slipped it into the document feeder. She pushed a button, and the machine whirred to life. "But you have to promise me you'll be careful."

"Of course, Mom." Cassie giggled.

Maggie handed her the copy. "I'm serious. When Rick called about the explosion, I..." Her eyes filled with tears.

Cassie pulled Maggie into another hug. "It's okay. I'm fine. Just a few cuts and bruises."

"I love you!" Maggie sniffed.

"I love you too." Cassie released the hug but gave Maggie's arm an extra squeeze. "But I gotta go open the store. You'll be in later?"

Maggie nodded. "Of course. Around eleven."

Cassie waved as she stepped out the door. She rushed back to her SUV and sped down the block to the parking lot behind her building. Taking the stairs two by two, Cassie was slightly out of breath when she reached her apartment to get Pumpkin.

"Rowr!" The cat voiced her disapproval at Cassie's absence.

"I know, I'm sorry. But let's go to the store now."

Pumpkin sat still and raised her head.

"C'mon, Pumpkin pie. I'm late."

The cat turned away.

"Fine. Stay here then." Cassie stepped back into the hallway, started to pull the door shut, but left it open for the last three inches. A paw appeared through the opening, followed by the big orange-and-white cat pushing it open wide enough so she could squeeze through.

Cassie smirked and shut the door behind Pumpkin. Kitties could be like two-year-olds sometimes.

The cat bounded down the stairs ahead of Cassie and waited at the back-door entrance of Olde Crow Primitives.

Cassie glanced across the hallway at The Book Nook door. Was Daniel at work already? She wanted to talk to him, but there wasn't time. She'd have to pop over once Maggie came in for her shift.

She unlocked her shop door and flipped the switch for the overhead lights. As she walked around to plug in all the mini lights for the displays, the scent of the fall candles delighted her senses. She'd never tire of that smell. The autumn décor accenting all the shelves and the leaf garlands hanging across the ceiling brought her joy. By the time she opened the front door at ten o'clock, she was relaxed and at peace.

Pumpkin jumped on the cash counter beside her as she turned on the computer. There were no customers yet. She might as well use this time to look through the open house list. She pulled it out of her purse and placed it on the counter. The cat plopped down and pawed at an upturned corner of the paper.

"Stop it." Cassie pushed the cat across the smooth surface of the counter. That only made her more determined. She inched forward and swatted the corner again.

"Pumpkin, no."

Pumpkin gave the corner one more swat for good measure. Cassie patted the cat's head as she studied the list.

There were eighteen entries. She studied each name, trying to recall what the people looked like. First was the couple with the snotty teens. They hadn't stayed long. She put a line through their entry.

She found the names of the couple who bought the house and another elderly couple she recalled and crossed them off the list. She remembered a few other couples, but nothing odd stood out about them. Most of them did a quick walk-through of the house and left. She put a line through their names as well.

By the time she reached the end, there were four entries left unmarked. Two people she couldn't put faces to, Harlan the military man, and Jarvis, the guy who didn't want to sign in.

Cassie looked at the old-fashioned wooden clock on the wall. Ten thirty. It was Wednesday, Officer Welby's day to be at the satellite office in Banford. Lexy would be there by now, working behind the reception counter.

She texted her friend.

Hey, hon! Trying to help Wesley. Want to research a name or two for me?

Hi! Sure. I'm bored. Welby locked himself in his office. I think he's playing games on his phone. LOL.

Cassie laughed. *I'm sure he is. First name is Jarvis Vinn. Second is Harlan Waller.*

K. I'll see what I can find.

Thanks!

She probably should've felt a bit guilty asking Lexy to use her position to find out information about the men, but on the other hand, Lexy was a superstar at finding things out through the internet.

She'd helped Cassie before, and those types of searches were legal. She wouldn't be breaching any confidence by doing so.

And technically, if the men had a record, it

wouldn't be secret knowledge.

In the end, Wesley needed their help. If Officer Welby wasn't going to do his job and conduct a proper investigation, didn't they have the right to interfere?

Cassie texted Rick next and asked about the other two names on the list. He texted back almost immediately.

He remembered them both, but neither person had stayed long, nor had they behaved suspiciously.

Now she just had to wait for Lexy to get back to her.

The bells on the front door jingled as two women entered the store. Cassie recognized one of them as a waitress from Hardcastle Pub and Restaurant, where she ate with Grams every Sunday morning before church.

She greeted the women, helped them find the right birthday present for a friend, and rang up their purchase at the cash register. They giggled at Pumpkin, still sprawled across the counter, and left with their gift in a paper bag bearing the shop logo and tied with a black-and-tan-checked ribbon.

Cassie's phone vibrated in her pocket before the door finished closing.

"Call me." It was Lexy. Had she already found something?

Cassie took advantage of the fact the store was empty again and phoned her friend.

"What's up?"

"Hey." Lexy spoke quietly, presumably so Officer Welby wouldn't overhear. "That Jarvis Vinn. Is he from Kemptville?" Lexy referred to a nearby town.

Cassie checked the sign-in sheet. "Yes."

"Okay. Guess where he works?"

"Where?"

"The quarry on the highway."

"So?"

"The quarry? Think, Cassie."

Cassie thought. Sand, stone dust, and different sizes of gravel came out of the quarry. She didn't see the connection. "I don't get it."

"How do they get the stone they need to make their aggregates?"

And then Cassie realized. "They blast it. The quarry has explosives."

"Exactly."

"Which means Jarvis Vinn had the means. What about a motive? What else did you find?"

Lexy sighed into the phone. "Not much, yet. He's had a number of speeding and parking offences, but no major charges for anything."

"Okay. Keep digging. In the meantime, I'll pay a visit to the quarry and see what I can find out."

"I want to help," Lexy said. "I'm off tomorrow.

Let's go together in the morning."
"Deal."
Cassie hung up and smiled.
Maybe they could help Wesley, after all.

Chapter 9

Cassie stood in the hallway between Olde Crow Primitives and The Book Nook, holding a paper bag with fresh sandwiches from Drummond's Bakery & Deli. Maggie had arrived promptly at eleven, and after an hour and a half of catching up with her and serving customers, Cassie took her lunch break.

Knowing Daniel couldn't leave his shop for long, Cassie decided to grab him a sandwich, too, and use it as kind of a peace offering. She hadn't spoken with him since the encounter with Spencer in her store. Sure, that was only yesterday, but it was the first time so many hours had passed in the last two months where she hadn't connected with Daniel.

She hesitated at the door, but Pumpkin raced

up and scratched the bottom of the frame.

"Hey!" Cassie nudged the cat with her foot. "Stop that."

Pumpkin meowed at her and scratched some more. Cassie opened the door, and Pumpkin waddled inside, heading straight for Daniel.

"Hey, Pumpkin." He knelt, holding his hand out toward her. She rubbed up against it and purred while he stroked her.

"Hi." Cassie held out the bag. "I brought you a sandwich from the deli. Hungry?"

Daniel stood. "Thanks." He turned and headed to the coffee bar. "Tea?"

"Sure. That'd be great." Her heart beat louder. Daniel was definitely not his cheery self. Had she been too harsh with him the other day?

Cassie made her way past the rows of old wooden bookshelves, arranged to create nooks along the length of the store, and took a seat in one of the comfy chairs. Low flames flickered in the fireplace, and the mantel was decorated with a number of fall decorations she had loaned him.

Above that hung a row of black-and-white photos Daniel had taken over the years. It always amazed her that in Toronto, Daniel was a famous photographer. She'd only ever known him as sweet, humble Daniel of Banford.

He returned with a mug of tea and held it out. She noticed it wasn't in the usual cat mug he reserved for her.

"Thank you." She instantly felt its warmth as she wrapped her hand around it.

"You're welcome." He set his own cup of coffee on the little table in front of them and took a seat in the next chair.

"Quiet in here." She pulled his sandwich out of the bag and handed it to him.

"Yeah. Slow day."

"For me, too."

He peeled the saran wrap off his sandwich and took a bite. Cassie stared at him, but he avoided her gaze. The tension in the air was as thick as the complete volume of Shakespeare's works.

After a couple more bites, Cassie couldn't stand it anymore. "Aren't you going to talk to me?"

"What do you mean?" He grabbed his coffee. "I've talked."

"Not like normal, and you know it. What's going on?"

"Nothing. I'm just back here in my store where I belong." He glanced up at her. "Isn't that what you told Spencer the other day?"

Cassie no longer felt remorse for her actions. "You deserved that."

"Oh, really?" Daniel raised his eyebrows.

"You were acting... possessive. He only came to check on me."

"Mm-hmm."

"He saved me from the fire, Daniel. You should have been more grateful."

"I am grateful. But checking on you, and checking you out, are two different things."

"He wasn't checking me out." Cassie sat up straighter. Her phone dug into her backside, so she pulled it out of her pocket and chucked it on the table. "He was being kind and considerate, unlike some people."

"I don't trust him."

"Oh, please. He's harmless. He was a total geek in high school."

"He didn't look like much of a geek to me."

Cassie took a breath. "Stop it. This is silly."

Daniel leaned his head to the side until his neck cracked. "I know what I saw."

"It doesn't matter anyway. Like I said, he was only checking on me. I have no interest in Spencer, nor does he have interest in me."

Daniel relaxed his shoulders. She thought she heard him mutter, "Good."

Cassie rolled her eyes and took another sip of tea. Time to change the subject. "Did you hear I'm helping Wesley?"

"You are? Don't you hate the guy?"

"Hate is a strong word. I don't hate anybody. I don't particularly like him, but he's not a murderer. And he's one of Rick's friends. I promised him I'd try to help."

Daniel nodded. "The police aren't investigating further?"

"Nope. They're sure they have their guy." Cassie went on to explain about the TNT in the trunk, the insurance money, and the timing of Wesley leaving Norma at the house alone. "And there aren't any other likely suspects."

"Except for the ones you've found?"

Cassie grinned. He knew her well. "Two so far. Both behaved strangely at the open house, and one of them has access to explosives."

He grabbed her hand. "Be careful."

"Of course. Why does everyone keep telling me that?"

Daniel stared at her with raised brows. "Really?"

Cassie giggled. She may or may not have a history of jumping headlong into potentially dangerous situations. "I'll be careful."

"Good." He squeezed her hand. "And I *am* grateful Muscle-head saved you. I don't know what I'd do without you."

"Muscle-head? Really?"

"What?" Daniel smirked and picked up his coffee again. "So, what's the plan of attack for your suspects?"

"Lexy's coming with me tomorrow to visit the quarry and inquire about Jarvis, the first suspect."

"You're not going to have a run-in with him, are

you?"

"Uh-uh. We're going to talk to his boss, about the explosives… or something." Cassie wasn't really sure what they should ask about.

"Oh—" He pointed at her shirt. "You have, uh…"

She looked down at the blob of mayonnaise sitting on her boob. "Ugh!" At her feet, Pumpkin licked a second blob from the rug.

"I'll get you a—" Daniel started to stand.

"No, no. You sit. I'll get something." Cassie headed to the coffee bar for a napkin, or ten.

She managed to wipe off most of the mayo, and then used a bit of water from the pod machine to scrub at the stain. Then she dampened another napkin to attack the spot on the rug.

When she returned, Daniel held her phone in his hand and was staring at the screen. His face was a funny shade of red.

"What are you doing?" she asked.

"Not interested, huh?"

"What are you talking about?" She snatched the phone from his hand. While she'd been at the coffee bar, Spencer had texted.

He asked her if she wanted to walk by the water and have a picnic dinner tomorrow evening.

Uh-oh.

"That doesn't mean anything." She flipped the curls off her shoulder.

"Sounds like a date to me." His shoulders

stiffened.

"First of all, I didn't know he was going to ask. Second, I never said anything to suggest I wanted him to ask. And *third*, why are you looking at my phone?"

Daniel shrugged. "First, I thought maybe it was important. Second, you left it sitting here in front of me. And *third*, I...I don't like the guy!"

Cassie put her hands on her hips. "Daniel Sawyer. Jealousy is not a good colour on you."

"I'm not jealous."

"You could have fooled me. You're acting like a schoolboy. He texted, big deal."

"It *is* a big deal. I told you, I don't trust him. There's something shifty about him."

"I find that hard to believe." Cassie felt her voice getting louder. "He just happens to be a good-looking guy who volunteers his time fighting fires, saving lives, and... teaching Sunday school kids at his church."

"So you admit you think he's good-looking. I knew it!" Daniel stood to his feet.

Cassie rolled her eyes. "You're impossible."

"And how do you know that other stuff about him? Clearly, you've been talking together."

"Actually, yes, we have." She decided to roll with it. "I went to the station last night to get more information from him about what caused the explosion and the fire."

The sides of Daniel's jaw pulsed. "You didn't tell me that."

"Of course not. I knew how you'd react."

"What else aren't you telling me then?"

"*Nothing.* There's nothing else to tell." Cassie huffed out the words. Pumpkin rubbed against her legs and meowed.

"What about the church thing? How did that come up?"

"In conversation."

"Interesting. Does *he* meet your requirements for dating? Does *he* love your God enough?"

"That's not fair."

"It's plenty fair. You've been stringing me along for months." Daniel's eyes narrowed.

"I've done no such thing. We're just friends. I can go out with whomever I please!"

"Fine. You have my blessing. Go out with him."

"I don't need your blessing. I'm *not* yours." Cassie regretted the words as soon as she said them, but she stood her ground, fists clenched at her side. "In fact, maybe I *will* go out with him."

She grabbed her phone from the table.

"What are you doing?"

"Texting him back." She spoke as she thumbed the message into the phone. "I'd love to go. You can pick me up at my apartment at six."

Daniel stormed off to the front of the store, and Cassie stomped to the hallway exit.

"Enjoy your dinner," Daniel called after her. "I hope he doesn't choke on his ego."

Cassie turned to look back at him. "The only one in danger of doing that is you. C'mon, Pumpkin."

The cat darted out into the hallway before Cassie slammed the door shut.

Tears welled up in her eyes, and she grabbed the stairway railing to steady herself as she tried to regain composure. She sat on the first step and buried her face in her hands. Pumpkin jumped up beside her and pushed her head against Cassie's side.

What had just happened? Cassie shook her head, trying to make sense of the conversation. This wasn't like Daniel. They'd never argued before. Now it was twice in one week.

Maybe later, after they'd both had time to cool down, she could try talking to Daniel again.

But then again, maybe that wouldn't work.

After all, she now had a date with Spencer the firefighter tomorrow night.

Chapter 10

"You did *what?*" Eyes wide, Lexy shot Cassie a surprised glance before returning her eyes to the road and steering her car around a wide curve. Cassie sat in the passenger seat.

"I know, I know. I'm dumb."

"You're not dumb, you're just..."

"Just what?"

"I don't know, impatient, maybe?" Lexy slowed as a car in front of her signalled to turn. "And Spencer Kingsley? Really?"

"Trust me. He's not like you remember him. I swear he's not even the same guy from high school."

"I doubt that." Lexy chuckled. "No one can change that much."

"Oh yeah? Let me find a picture." Cassie

searched the fire department on her phone. Hopefully there'd be a volunteer firefighter group photo or something.

"Did Daniel really get that angry?"

"Yes."

"Wow. He's got it worse than I thought."

Cassie ignored Lexy's comment and continued scrolling.

"Find a picture yet?" Lexy peered at Cassie's phone.

"Nope, still looking. I'm looking for—"

"What? Why is your face so red?" Lexy tried to look at the screen again.

"Well. I found one." Cassie looked down at the firefighter fundraiser calendar advertised on the home page of the station's site. On the cover, a fireman wearing nothing but the pants of his uniform stared back at her. It was Spencer. His chest protruded from behind the red suspenders, sparkling with sweat. He held an axe and... wow. He was ripped.

She held up the phone so Lexy could see.

Her eyes bulged out of her head as much as Spencer's muscles bulged in the photo. *That's* Spencer?" The car swerved.

"Yup." Cassie smirked. "Eyes on the road."

Lexy straightened the vehicle and blinked slowly. "Woah."

"Uh-huh."

"He certainly picked the right profession." Lexy gave her head a shake. "That dude is *smokin' hot.*"

Cassie groaned, and Lexy giggled.

"I was going to try to get you guys together." Cassie put her phone away. "He's a sweet guy. I think you'd be a good match."

"Thanks, but kinda late now. Besides, I have someone in mind."

"You do? Who?"

"There's the quarry." Lexy pointed at a sign ahead.

"You're changing the subject."

"Yes, I am." Lexy grinned. She drove down the gravel driveway and parked in front of the scale house. A dump truck driver waved as he steered his truck off the scale.

Cassie hopped out and entered the tiny one-room office.

"How can I help?" an older gentleman asked. He had a full head of wavy grey hair and laughter lines around his eyes.

"Hi. I'd like to speak to someone about, uh… I'd like to speak to a manager, please." What *was* she going to ask him about?

"Sure." The gentleman picked up the phone and had a brief conversation. "Okay. Follow this road out to the east side of the quarry." He pointed out the window at a gravel lane. "Over the hill you'll come to a blue trailer. You can talk to Ray in there."

"Thank you."

"And watch for the trucks."

"I will, thanks." Cassie hopped back into the vehicle beside Lexy and pointed in the direction they should go.

Lexy drove down the lane, creating a big cloud of dust that followed behind them. As promised, over the hill was an old blue trailer, similar to what one might see at a temporary construction site. It sat on a rocky ledge, overlooking a huge, deep quarry. She parked the car again, and this time they both hopped out.

"I still don't know what to ask," Cassie admitted.

"Trust God. He'll give you the words." Lexy smiled and patted her friend's shoulder.

Cassie said a silent prayer and knocked on the office door.

"Come in!" a rough voice called from inside.

The girls let themselves in and came face-to-face with a burly man in his fifties. His work pants and shirt were covered with a layer of dust, as was everything in his office. A white hard hat sat on a mess of papers on his desk.

"How can I help you ladies?" He rubbed his cheek, leaving a clean spot amid the dirt.

"Hi. My name is Cassie." She stretched out her hand.

"Ray." He shook it, leaving a gritty residue on her fingers. He nodded at Lexy, who smiled back.

Cassie swallowed and forced herself to speak. "I'm not sure if you've heard, but a house in Banford burned down a couple of days ago."

"Oh, yeah. I did hear something about that." He sat on the edge of his desk and crossed his arms in front of him. "A lady died, right?"

"Yes."

"So, how can I help you?"

Cassie clasped her hands in front of her and squeezed them together. "I helped conduct an open house at the property before the fire. As it happens, one of your employees came through that open house, but behaved a little, uh, suspiciously." Honesty was the best policy, right?

"One of my guys?"

"I don't know if he has anything to do with it, but there was an explosion prior to the fire. It was deliberately set."

"And you think my guy may be involved?"

"Possibly."

"Are you with the police?"

"Sort of," Lexy interjected.

"But we're mostly looking into it for a friend." Cassie didn't want Lexy to get in trouble. Better to play it safe.

"Which employee of mine are we talking about here?"

The girls exchanged glances. Should they say? Cassie had been in similar situations before. She wasn't too eager to go down the path of accusing someone without proof—again.

Lexy nodded.

"Jarvis Vinn," Cassie answered.

"Oh." Ray scratched the scruff on his face. "He is a bit of a strange one."

"Can you check if any explosives are missing?" Cassie suddenly felt hopeful. "That could be a place to start."

"Let me talk to Tommy. He's our blasting guy." Ray picked up the phone and spoke loudly into the receiver. Then he hung up. "Grab a couple of hard hats and follow me. Tommy's going to meet us at the blasting house where we keep the explosives."

The girls grabbed two yellow hats from hooks near the door, giggled at each other as they put them on, and followed Ray as he walked down a steep hill into the quarry. Below, a huge machine crushed stone and poured the resulting gravel into large piles via a long conveyer belt. Drivers lined up as a couple of backhoes loaded the stone into the truck beds. Massive clouds of dust rose into the sky.

Ray turned on a path that led to the outer edge of the quarry. A solid steel shed stood within a securely fenced area.

He unlocked the chain on the gate and let the

girls follow him into the enclosed space. "You can't go into the shed, I'm afraid. It's one of the safety and security protocols."

"Sure, no problem." Cassie nodded. She had no idea the area would be so locked down. "Who all has keys and access to the shed, Ray?"

He fiddled with one of the two locks on the blasting shed door. "Only me and Tommy." He nodded his head to point up the lane. "Here he comes now."

Tommy, equally aged and covered in dirt, entered the gate. "Ladies." He smiled at them. "What's up, Boss?"

"Just checking the inventory. Has anything gone missing?"

"Of course not. You know if I don't track every ounce of this stuff I could lose my licence."

"Yeah, yeah. How's about you check anyway?"

Tommy grumbled and opened the other lock. He stepped into the shed and came out a few moments later with a clipboard. "S'all good."

"You sure?" Ray narrowed his eyes and studied Tommy's face.

"I'm sure. I checked it this morning, and everything is still in its place."

"All right. Thanks, Tommy."

Tommy grumbled as he locked the shed back up. The girls followed Ray out of the fenced area and up the hill.

"There you go. Nothing here is missing."

"Thank you for checking." Cassie wiped some dust from her eyelashes.

"When did you say that fire happened?" Ray shouted over the noise of a truck climbing a steep hill out of the quarry.

"Tuesday."

"Oh! Well, it couldn't have been Vinn anyway. He was here at work all day."

"Are you sure?" Lexy asked.

"Positive. He works the crusher, and the other guy who does it was off. It ran all day, so I know he couldn't have been gone."

"Okay, well thank you very much for your help." Cassie handed him the hard hats and waved at the man before he returned into his work trailer.

"Ugh. I need a shower." Lexy frowned as she climbed into her vehicle. As she sat, a small cloud of dust puffed up into the air.

The same happened to Cassie. She giggled. "Isn't there a Charlie Brown character like us?"

"I think he was cleaner."

As they drove off and returned to the highway, the girls stayed silent.

Cassie was grateful Ray was so helpful, but unfortunately it meant the road to Jarvis Vinn was a dead end.

Lexy must have sensed Cassie's distress, because she leaned over and patted her leg. "Don't worry. We still have the military guy to look into."

"True." Lexy was right. Jarvis may have been strange and tried to avoid signing in, but the really peculiar behaviour came from Harlan Waller. He was the one who spent all that time in the cellar.

The cellar where the explosion started.

"What have you found out about him so far?" Cassie asked.

"Not much. But he works at the army base south of Ottawa."

"Hmm… fancy a ride into the city after we get cleaned up? I'll see if I can get Grams to cover the store with Maggie."

"Sure! I'll drive."

Cassie wiped some dust from the dashboard. "I can drive. I don't mind."

"No, I'll drive." Lexy winked at her. "We have to make sure we're back in time for your hot date."

Cassie groaned.

Chapter 11

After a quick shower, Cassie dressed and brought Pumpkin down to the store. She knew the cat would much rather stay there with Grams and Maggie than to be cooped up by herself in the apartment.

Grams had agreed to take a shift for the afternoon, as Cassie knew she would. She used to think she was taking advantage of her grandmother, but the truth was Grams loved to revisit her old store. Many customers still knew her by name, and she enjoyed meeting ones who didn't.

Cassie once asked her grandmother if she regretted retiring when she did, but Grams was quick to reassure her she was happy. There were lots of headaches that came with running a store and rental units, and if she could come in and help once in a while, she could do the part she loved without all the nonsense, as she called it.

And it turned out to be a huge help to Cassie. Especially when trying to find a murderer.

"Have fun, dear!" Grams waved. "Oh! But be careful!"

"Thanks, Grams!"

"Don't forget to be back in time for your date," Maggie teased.

"How did you—?"

Maggie wiggled the phone in her hand. Good ole' Lexy. Cassie grimaced.

"Date? What date?" Grams asked.

"Never mind." Cassie rolled her eyes. "I'm sure Maggie will fill you in."

Maggie grinned and waved as Cassie headed out the back.

Cassie paused in the hallway. She hadn't talked to Daniel since their argument more than twenty-four hours ago. Add most of Tuesday, and that made almost two full days she'd spent without him this week. Her stomach churned.

She didn't like that.

And now she had that stupid date with Spencer. She'd thought a number of times about cancelling, but for some reason she didn't feel right about it. Normally, Thursday was her Bible study night, but it had been cancelled this week because of Thanksgiving, so she couldn't even use that as an excuse. When they went out, she'd be honest about her situation and dissuade him from pursuing her further. Maybe she could even steer him toward Lexy.

Speaking of Lexy, she should arrive at any moment. Cassie stopped staring at The Book Nook door and went outside. Probably not a wiser choice, as she now had to pass by the front entrance of the bookstore and decide whether or not to look into the window. Her heart pounded as she approached.

She opted not to look in.

Cassie turned the corner and crossed the parking lot. If she waited in the far corner at the yellow-leaf-covered picnic table, she would be out of sight from the rest of the bookshop windows.

Crisp leaves crunched beneath her feet as she crossed the lawn to the table. She sat and pulled her cardigan tightly around her to prevent the cold breeze from getting through.

What was she doing? She had the day off, and she was spending it chasing dead-end leads instead of getting her butt into the store and apologizing to Daniel.

Or should he be apologizing to her? They *weren't* dating. He had no right to get so upset with her. Or to be so jealous. Did he?

And where did he get off accusing her of

stringing him along? She'd done no such thing.

A thought struck her. How would she feel if a gorgeous blonde hit on Daniel? And what if he made plans to go out with her?

She shuddered at the thought. Or was it the breeze? She pulled her sweater tighter again.

For now, Daniel was only her friend. And it had to stay that way, until God told her otherwise. And the last thing He'd told her was to wait.

For the next few minutes, she contemplated whether or not she'd messed that up with her behaviour. Accepting the date with Spencer was wrong on so many levels.

Lexy pulled into the parking lot before Cassie could beat herself up more about her decision. She was grateful for the distraction.

"Ready to go?" Lexy put the window down and smiled at Cassie as she approached the car. Her hair was pulled into a cute updo, and her makeup was fresh and bright. She'd put on a fun red lipstick that matched her sweater.

"You look cute." Cassie climbed into the vehicle. "What's the occasion?"

"Uh... military base? Hello!"

Cassie laughed. Of course Lexy would have thought of that. She hung onto the door as Lexy zoomed out of the parking lot. "What's the hurry?"

"If we find out what we need at the base soon enough, we'll have time to go shopping. Maybe get you a new outfit for your date tonight."

"Ugh. Stop calling it a date."

"What would you call it?"

Cassie groaned. "A blunder."

"Wow. I could only hope to make such blunders."

"Stop it." Cassie teasingly swatted Lexy's arm. "Speaking of dates, you still haven't told me who you have your eye on."

"And I won't tell you now, either." Lexy lifted her chin. "You'll find out when I'm ready. It might not matter anyway."

"If you say so." Cassie stared out the window as they drove down the highway toward Ottawa.

Since Cassie didn't want to talk about Daniel or Spencer, and Lexy didn't want to talk about her latest crush, the girls turned up the music and sang loudly together the rest of the way to the city.

Almost an hour later, they pulled into the army base on the southeast side of Ottawa.

"It's in the middle of nowhere." Lexy ducked her head under the visor to get a better look at the large white building in front of them.

"Where do we go in?" Cassie studied the high, black fence surrounding the building and grounds.

Lexy drove the length until they came to a tall gate with white bars. A security officer waited in a booth on the other side. "I'm guessing here."

"Uh-oh." Cassie sighed. "Somehow I don't think

this will be as easy to get into as the quarry."

Lexy pulled the vehicle into a parking space. "What do they do here, anyway?"

"Some kind of encryption or communications interception."

"Yeah. Definitely not getting in."

The girls got out and made their way to the gate.

The security officer, a balding man in his forties who, based on the size of his stomach, had a lot of spare time to eat while manning his booth, met them at the gate. "How are you today?"

"Very good, thank you." Lexy pulled a piece of hair from her updo and twirled it between her fingers.

Cassie rolled her eyes. Not. Going. To. Work.

"How can I help you?"

Honesty, Cassie thought. It worked at the quarry, didn't it? "We have some questions about someone who works here. Is there a manager, or uh, a sergeant we can talk to?"

The man chuckled. "You mean a captain? Or a major?"

"Yes, that's it." Cassie felt her cheeks warm.

"Do you have an appointment?" The guard held onto his belt with both hands and rocked on his heels. "I don't recall seeing two ladies' names on my list."

"No." Lexy twirled her hair again. "Do we need

one?"

"Absolutely. No one can get in without getting pre-approved and being put on the list."

"Isn't there someone you could call right now, to get us approved?" Another hair twirl.

The guard laughed outright this time. "No can do. The pre-approval process requires security and background checks. That process can take a few weeks."

Cassie groaned.

"Ugh." Lexy finally let go of her hair. "There's nothing you can do?"

He shook his head.

"Maybe *you* can help us," Cassie decided. "Do you know a Harlan Waller who works here?"

"I'm not at liberty to discuss our staff, ma'am."

"Oh, come on!" Lexy stomped her foot. "We know he works here. Can't you just tell us if he was here on Tuesday? Or if his rank allows him access to explosives? We're trying to solve a murder here!"

"Pardon me?" The guard raised his eyebrows and took a step back. "I think you ladies should leave."

Cassie ran her hand over her face and sighed in frustration. She took another breath to steady herself and looked directly into the guard's eyes. "Please, sir. It's very important. An innocent man might go to jail. We're only trying to help him."

"Trying to help? Or trying to cause trouble? It sounds to me like you think Lieutenant Waller might be a suspect."

"Ha! So he does work here." Lexy grinned.

Cassie elbowed her friend in the side. "If you could just tell us if he was here on Tuesday, there'd be no question. He'd have an alibi."

"You need to leave right now, or I'm going to call for backup."

"Backup? Really?" Lexy huffed and put her hands on her hips. "Are a couple of girls behind a twenty-foot gate too much for you to handle on your own?"

"C'mon, Lex." Cassie tugged on her friend's arm as Security Man pushed a button on his radio and opened his mouth to speak.

As soon as they stepped away, he let go of the radio button and returned to his booth.

"What a waste of time!" Lexy climbed in the vehicle and slammed the door shut after her.

Cassie seconded the door slamming motion. "We're no further ahead at all."

"And if Mr. Harlan Waller is involved, it will be pretty tricky to prove it." Lexy backed out of the parking space and zipped toward the road. "At least there's some good news."

"There is?" Cassie tugged on her seatbelt to tighten it.

"Now we have time to go shopping!"

Chapter 12

Spencer Kingsley arrived promptly at six o'clock bearing a box of chocolate caramels. He wore jeans and a fitted navy shirt with the top few buttons undone, revealing a grey T-shirt underneath. Despite her lack of eagerness for the date, Cassie's heart beat a bit faster at the visually appealing man in front of her.

Lexy was right. He was definitely in the right profession.

The temperature had dropped since the afternoon, so after Cassie pulled on her brown knee-high boots, she added a puffy red vest over her brown sweater and grabbed a pair of brown fuzzy mittens.

"Mittens? Really?" Spencer smirked.

"What? It's getting chilly."

Spencer gently took the mittens from her hand and tossed them back into the basket she'd grabbed them from. "If your hands get cold, I'll warm them up." He winked.

Cassie swallowed. It sounded like the kind of corny line Wesley would offer up, but Spencer could definitely pull it off. Regardless, as he headed out the door, she reached back and grabbed the mittens.

As they crossed the parking lot to retrieve the picnic basket from Spencer's green roadster, the back of Cassie's neck tingled. Was Daniel watching from the book shop window?

She refused to look. What if he was? She wouldn't give him the satisfaction of letting him know she saw him. In fact, she didn't care if he was watching. There was no way she was going to look. Stringing him along, indeed.

Cassie turned around.

He was there, in the window, like she suspected. His face was as long as the days in July. Her chest started to hurt a little. She pressed on it with her hand and turned back to Spencer.

"I hope you like chicken." Spencer pulled an actual wooden picnic basket and a woolly plaid blanket out of the passenger seat. "And pasta."

"I do." Cassie forced a smile. Now wasn't the time to think about Daniel. "Where do you want to sit?" She looked across the road at the park beside the locks.

"If you don't mind walking a little bit, I know the perfect spot." The veins in his forearm popped out as he held the large basket. His long hair teased his shoulders.

"Sure. I'm game." She followed him across the street, and across the top of the first set of locks.

He led her down a trail that followed the river to the end of a spit. There, he set the basket on a flat rock under a large maple, grabbed the blanket from under his arm, and spread it out on a bed of freshly fallen leaves.

"I thought we could watch the sunset while we eat." He sat and patted the blanket.

She couldn't help but smile. "This is one of my favourite spots." She sat and crossed her legs criss-cross apple sauce.

"Really?" He chuckled.

"I come here to journal and spend time with God." Heat rose to her cheeks. Was that too personal? "It's a great spot to watch birds too."

"You're a birder?"

"Yes." She nodded, surprised he knew the correct term, and even more surprised he didn't tease her for it, like Daniel often did.

"My aunt and uncle are pretty serious birders." Spencer opened the basket and pulled out dishes and cutlery. "They travel around the world to go on birding expeditions."

"How amazing!" Cassie couldn't help but gush. "I'd love to do that."

"Maybe someday you will." He handed her a plate, his green eyes sparkling in the remaining sunlight.

"Do you like to travel?"

"I love it. I backpacked Europe after high school and have made a point since then to take a big trip at least every two years. I've been to Australia and New Zealand, a few spots in Asia, and Central America. There are a ton of birds there."

"I went to Europe for a couple of months." Cassie took the lids off of the containers as Spencer placed them on the blanket. "Oh my goodness, this smells amazing. Where did you get it?"

He put his hand on his chest. "Chez Kingsley, of course."

"*You* made this?" Cassie eyed the spread of crispy fried chicken, two types of creamy pasta salads, and roasted potatoes.

"Cooking is a hobby of mine." He dug a spoon into the first salad and put some on her plate.

"Takeout is a hobby of mine." Cassie grinned.

The two filled their plates, and then their tummies, as the sun set behind the water. She'd have to add "good cook" to the list of Spencer's attributes.

They talked about high school, old friends, and about returning to Banford. Then they each shared how they came to know God.

While in Europe, Spencer learned to come out of his shell and not be so shy. By the time he'd returned to Canada, he'd had a better sense of who he was.

Unfortunately, that had also worked against him in university. He'd started to work out, build muscle, and get attention from girls. By the end of his first year, he'd become quite the partier and had earned a reputation as a wild guy.

Then things went south in his third year when he was drinking with a group of friends at a nearby lake. One of his buddies ended up getting killed in a cliff diving accident. Even though there were a dozen people there that night, Spencer had felt responsible and was forced to step back and take a good look at his life.

In one of his classes, his table mate had talked to him about God. Shortly after, Spencer had gone with him to a campus Bible study, and within three months, he'd turned his life over to God.

It didn't bring back his friend, but it'd helped Spencer deal with the loss, accept forgiveness, and see the bigger picture of his life.

Cassie shared with him her story about Chris and how she'd returned to Banford after the wedding was cancelled. She told him how Grams helped her get back on her feet and redirected her to the way she was brought up—to love God, and to serve Him.

Cassie was surprised at how easy it was to talk with Spencer, and she couldn't help but note how nice it was to have God be such a natural part of the conversation. By the time they finished the apple crumble he'd made for dessert, it was nearing seven thirty.

Spencer packed the containers into the basket. "If it's okay with you, I'd like to stop by Mrs. Dingham's Antique Shop before she closes at eight."

"Sure. I haven't been there in a while." She stood so he could shake out the blanket. She grabbed an end to help him fold it, and after a few lengthwise folds, she brought her end toward his. Their hands touched, and their faces were closer than she anticipated.

Cassie felt heat rise to her cheeks and quickly took a step back. What was going on here? She was supposed to apologize to him tonight for misleading him, and to clarify she only wanted to be friends. She had feelings for Daniel, and she needed to be honest with Spencer. She needed to be fair.

And she had no time to waste.

"Spencer, I need to—"

"Listen!" He pointed across the river into the darkness. An owl hooted and Spencer imitated the call. "Who cooks for you? Who cooks for you all?"

He grinned. "A barred owl, right?"

"Yes! I'm impressed." Cassie led the way back down the path to the park, using her phone flashlight to guide the way.

"See? I'm not completely bird ignorant."

"There's been a pair hanging out there for the last two years. Sometimes in the winter, they show up in the park at night."

"You've seen them?"

"A few times. Once I was able to get right under the tree, and I could see the shadowed outline of the owl in the moonlight."

"Amazing."

Cassie smiled. She knew he meant it.

After they crossed through the park, Spencer had her wait on the sidewalk while he ran across the street to put the basket and blanket into his car. In the park, lights at the top of the lampposts glowed, and Cassie couldn't help but notice the only other people around were couples.

The car door slammed and drew her attention. As Spencer jogged back across the street, she was struck again by his handsome form. God did good work with Spencer.

They headed down the street to Mrs. Dingham's shop, less than a block away. Cassie wore her mittens but also shoved her hands in her vest pockets for good measure. Then she wouldn't have to worry about him trying to hold her hand.

Mrs. Dingham's Antiques was one of Banford's staple shops. A covered porch filled with pressback chairs, milk cans, wagon wheels, and old hand farming tools ran the length of the old wooden building. It was decorated with pumpkins and orange lights.

Spencer held the door open for Cassie. Mrs. Dingham sat on a stool behind a counter. Her white hair was pulled into a neat bun on top of her head, and the glasses on her nose were as wiry as the thin body they adorned.

"Cassie, my dear. How are you?"

"Hi, Mrs. Dingham. I'm good, thanks. This is my friend, Spencer." She held her hand out toward him.

"I know Spencer." Mrs. Dingham lowered her spectacles and peeked over them. "He's one of my regulars."

"Hi, Alice. You look beautiful tonight." Spencer winked and greeted her warmly.

The old lady blushed.

"Any new records this week?" He peeked behind the counter.

"None yet. But don't worry, I'll be sure to save them for you if they come in."

"Records?" Cassie raised an eyebrow.

"Vinyl. Especially from the seventies."

Cassie smiled. Was there no end to Spencer's revelations? Just when she thought she'd had him figured out, he threw something else at her she found surprising. She hadn't figured him to be a record collector.

"Do we have time to look around?" Spencer checked his phone.

"Of course, dears." Mrs. Dingham pulled some knitting out from behind the counter. "Take all the time you need."

Spencer followed Cassie through the skinny aisles as they browsed the tables cluttered with antiques and collectibles. There were tables dedicated to glassware, porcelain dishes, old clocks, vases, costume jewelry, and sterling silver tea sets. Beyond the tables stood a row of old dressers and cabinets. Spencer and Cassie took their time touching items and looking them over. This store definitely represented another time.

In the next row, Cassie stopped to admire a display of teacups and saucers.

She picked up a white one with little burgundy flowers painted on the fine bone china. It was from one of the Royal Albert collections.

"I'm more of a whiskey kind of guy." Spencer stood before a table full of old bottles and held a red-capped one labelled "Old Log Cabin." A red banner across the yellowed label declared it to be straight bourbon whiskey.

"Cool." Cassie took the bottle from him and studied it. Above the red banner was a picture of an old log cabin, nestled between tall evergreen trees. "I've never seen a bottle like this."

"You like it?" Spencer did a double take.

"It's pretty." Cassie brushed her thumb across the red cap. "It would look nice in a display."

Spencer looked at his phone. "It's after eight. We'd better go."

They squeezed out of the aisle and headed back to the front of the store.

"Good night, Alice." Spencer waved and touched the small of Cassie's back as he led her to the door. His hand felt strong.

"'Night you two."

"Bye." Cassie stepped out into the crisp night air.

"Walk by the water?" Spencer held his hand out to her, but Cassie pulled her mittens out of her vest pockets and put them on.

"Sure."

They headed back up the street and into the park again. The few remaining boats of the season bobbed in the river, their lights shimmering across the water.

This time, Spencer and Cassie followed the river the other direction and walked alongside the lock system. For a while, they walked in silence, enjoying the autumn night air and God's beauty. Then they sat on top of a picnic table overlooking the water and talked more about family, life, travelling, and what they each enjoyed most about their churches.

Before Cassie realized, it was close to ten thirty.

When she told Spencer it was time for her to go home, he not only walked her back, he walked her right to her apartment door.

"I had a great time." He rested his hand on the door jamb above her and leaned in.

"Me too. Thanks."

He leaned in farther, and Cassie was sure he was going to kiss her, so she shifted her head to the side and gave him a hug instead.

His grip was firm but gentle. His muscles were larger than Daniel's, and it felt different. His hair smelled a bit like citrus.

Inside her apartment, she kicked off her boots and brought Pumpkin to the couch for a cuddle, where she spent some time mulling the evening over. What she thought would be a disaster had turned out to be a pleasant night.

Spencer was kind and clearly loved God. She didn't expect to find such a warm, caring soul under his strapping exterior. He seemed like a good man.

It wasn't until she turned in for the night that she remembered she'd forgotten to talk to Spencer about only being friends.

Chapter 13

Friday. Five days since the Banford Bird Club had spotted the northern parula in the woods. Even so, Cassie couldn't resist trekking through the forest before work. The chances were next to nothing the bird would still be around, but there hadn't been much time this week to check for it. She figured it was worth a shot, but once again came up empty-handed.

Regardless, the walk had done her good. It was nice to spend some time in God's creation before her workday. Especially since she woke feeling confused about her feelings for Daniel and Spencer. She'd needed to clear her head.

It had worked for the time being. But now, as she dusted the shelves and displays in Olde Crow

Primitives, the men continually appeared in her mind's eye.

Spencer had been a pleasant surprise. He was everything a good Christian girl could hope for. But Daniel was sweet too. And kind, and... wonderful. And no one made Cassie's heart beat the way Daniel did. But he wasn't a Christian—yet.

Wait. That's what God had spoken to her. But wait for what? Or whom? He hadn't been specific. And her heart was anything but a reliable judge at the moment.

"Deep in thought, dear?" Grams appeared, arms crossed in front of her. She was working the morning shift today.

"Huh?"

Grams pointed at the feather duster in Cassie's hand. "You've been dusting the same shelf for the last five minutes."

Cassie's cheeks warmed. "Oh."

"Thinking about Spencer, perhaps?"

"No." Cassie turned and dusted another shelf. "Maybe."

"He seems like a nice young man."

"He is."

"But so is Daniel."

Cassie nodded but continued to face away from her grandmother. This wasn't helping.

"Daniel isn't speaking to me at the moment."

"So I've heard." Cassie could feel Grams's eyes

boring into the back of her neck. "Have you apologized to him yet?"

Cassie turned. "No, nor has he apologized to me. It's a two-way street."

"But someone needs to cross first." Grams pursed her lips into a thin line and raised her eyebrows into the wrinkles in her forehead.

Cassie sighed and slumped her shoulders. "I will. In time. I have to figure out this stuff in my head first."

"Take it to God, honey. Always take it to God."

"I know. I have." She turned back to dusting. Had she? She'd been talking to God about it, or at least remembering what He'd said. But had she really asked Him what He thought? Had she left her relationships in His hands? If she was this confused about everything, and so bogged down by thoughts about Daniel and Spencer, maybe it sat in her own uncapable hands, instead.

She made a mental note to spend more time with God after work, maybe journaling by the water and handing everything back to Him. It was all about trust. Her favourite verse ran through her head again. She needed to trust His leading and not lean on her own understanding. If she acknowledged Him, He would direct her paths.

The door chimes rang, and Rick appeared at the front of the store, dressed in his work suit and holding a cardboard tray with three coffee cups.

"Good morning, Sis. Grams."

Cassie stepped out from behind a tall wooden display case. He handed her one of the cups. The aroma of the Earl Grey tea instantly soothed her. "Thanks!"

"Thank you, dear." Grams turned her head so he could kiss her cheek.

"Any headway with the case?" He set the empty tray on the counter.

"No. Lexy did a search but wasn't able to find out any more about Harlan." Cassie walked to the cash counter and set the feather duster beside the tray. Pumpkin immediately lunged from her basket and attacked the feathers.

"Silly cat." Rick gave her a scratch on the head. "I might be able to help."

"Please do. I'm at a loss."

"Wesley had his lawyer call me this morning. Guess who's in the will?"

"The will? Who?" Grams asked.

"Helen Gallagher."

"Who?" Cassie wracked her brain, trying to recall where she'd heard the name before.

"Of course." Grams gasped. "Norma's nurse."

Rick took a sip of his coffee, his grin protruding on either side of his cup. "I think I just solved the case."

Cassie laughed. "Slow down, Sherlock. It doesn't mean anything, yet."

"But it's a good lead, right?" He stood tall and tugged on the edge of his coat jacket.

"Yes. Good boy." Cassie patted the top of his head.

Rick panted like a dog.

"Oh, you two!" Grams shook her head.

"I gotta head back to the office. Go work your magic!" Rick turned and breezed out the door, almost knocking over a customer on her way in.

"Thanks!" Cassie called after him. She turned to the customer. "Sorry about that."

The woman smiled sweetly at Cassie and continued into the store to look around.

Cassie turned to Grams. "What do you know about Helen?" She kept her voice down.

"Not much." Grams shrugged. "I've met her a handful of times. She's been Norma's nurse for years, living at the house with her for the last five. But every time I visited, she made herself scarce. I think she has a couple of adult children living in the area, but I can't be certain."

A couple of other women entered the store. Cassie waved as they headed to the wooden sign display at the rear of the shop. "Let me know if you need help finding anything."

They smiled and nodded.

Cassie plucked a feather from Pumpkin's mouth and tucked the duster under the counter out of the cat's reach. She meowed in protest.

"If Helen lived with Norma, then she'd be out of a job and a home when the house sold, correct?" Cassie drummed her fingers on the counter.

"Well, yes. But she already was. Don't forget, Norma had already moved into the villa. But Helen went with her—sort of. She got her old job back working in the long-term care wing."

"But she had to find a new place to live, right?"

"She must have."

"And I'm guessing she's not making as much as she did working for Norma?"

Grams scratched Pumpkin's ears. "That, I don't know."

"Either way, add in the fact she stood to inherit, and I think we have a motive."

"But an explosion?" Grams winced. "I don't know if she'd be capable of such an act at her age. Or at all."

"Money is a strong motivator. It makes people do all sorts of things they wouldn't otherwise do." Cassie thought back to another recent scenario she'd uncovered in Banford at the fishing derby.

"I suppose you're right, dear." Grams frowned, and her eyes watered. "I'm so glad you agreed to help Wesley. Norma would be heartbroken to know he sat in jail accused of murdering her."

Cassie reached out and rubbed Grams's arm. She'd forgotten to think of Grams's feelings through all this. Norma had been a close friend.

Cassie had to help Wesley, not only for Wesley's sake, but because he was Norma's son. If anything, she had to do it for Grams. "I'm doing everything I can."

Grams took Cassie's hand in her own and squeezed it. "Thank you. But be careful."

"I will."

"What's the next step?"

Cassie glanced at the old clock on the wall. "Hmm. I think it's time I stopped in to visit Mrs. Cranston at the villa, don't you?" Cassie said, referring to an elderly parishioner from their church who lived in the long-term care building.

Grams clasped her hands together. "That's a great plan."

"I'll leave after one, when Maggie comes in for her shift."

"Don't forget to bring her favourite cookies!"

Cassie smiled.

That meant she could also get herself a doughnut.

Chapter 14

"How do we find Helen? We don't even know what she looks like." Lexy slammed the car door and followed Cassie across the parking lot at the Hudson Retirement Villa.

Lexy took the afternoon off as she'd put in extra hours this week at the municipal office, working overtime at the police office to assist Officer Welby with the murder paperwork. Cassie was grateful for her company.

"Good question. Why do I never think about these things?"

"It's still a good idea." Lexy patted her friend's back as they walked up the sidewalk.

A gardener started a leaf blower and cleared the walk ahead of them. They ceased talking for the moment and skirted around him. Cassie scanned the grounds.

The retirement villa was rather large for the size of Banford, but people came from all over to live here. It consisted of two three-storey apartment buildings for seniors, and a two-storey long-term care building for those who could no longer care for themselves. Grams lived in one of the apartment buildings.

Cassie balanced the plate of cookies on her hand as Lexy pressed the button at the front door. A second later, the door buzzed, allowing them to open it and access the building.

"Can you please remind me what room Mrs. Cranston is in?" Cassie asked as she signed her and Lexy's names into the visitor log.

The plump red-haired lady behind the desk flipped through a binder. "Two-oh-two."

"Thanks." Cassie put down the pen.

"Is Helen working here today?" Lexy asked the lady. "Helen Gallagher? She's a friend of mine."

Red bangs fell into the woman's face as she nodded. "Yup. I can page her for you." She picked up the phone receiver.

"No, no." Lexy waved her hand. "That's fine. I'll find her later."

"Sure." The woman returned her gaze to her computer screen.

Cassie glanced at Lexy. They needed more information. Lexy shrugged.

"Is she working in the Cedar Wing today?" Cassie asked the woman.

"Cedar?" She scrunched her face. "She doesn't work in Cedar. She's in Maple."

"Oh right. That's what I meant. Thanks!" Cassie turned and walked away.

"Good one." Lexy nudged Cassie.

"It narrows it down to half a floor, anyway."

"Which wing is Mrs. Cranston in?"

Cassie shrugged. "I'm not sure. Let's find out."

The girls took the elevator to the second floor and entered the Oak Wing to get to room 202. The door was open, so they walked into the double occupancy room. A frail, elderly woman was asleep in the bed across from Mrs. Cranston's, but Mrs. Cranston's bed was vacant.

"She's not here." Cassie's shoulders slumped.

"Let's leave the cookies for her with a note. Maybe we can check back after we find Helen."

Cassie crossed the room and set the plate of cookies on a small table beside a comfy corner chair. As she set it down, she noticed a newsletter on the table entitled *Hudson Villa Weekly*. She picked it up and flipped through the six or seven pages it contained.

"Lex! Look." She held out the newsletter.

There was a photo of a resident sitting behind a big birthday cake with the number ninety-five on it. She was surrounded by nurses, smiling for the photo. According to the caption, the nurse in the top left of the photo was Helen Gallagher—a tall, slim woman in her sixties or so. She had short spiky hair and wore dark-rimmed glasses.

"Now we know who we're looking for." Lexy grinned.

Cassie returned the newsletter to the table and scrawled a quick note to Mrs. Cranston. When she finished, she followed Lexy to the elevator. "What should we say to Helen when we see her?"

Lexy pushed the first floor button to get to the Maple Wing. "No idea. Think of something."

As the girls exited the elevator, Lexy grabbed Cassie's arm. "There she is right there."

Helen leaned over a counter at the nurse's station, gabbing with another employee.

"Here goes nothing." Cassie marched forward. "Helen?"

The woman turned her head. "Yes?"

"Hi. I wanted to offer my condolences for the death of your boss, Mrs. Clarkson."

"Oh." She stepped away from the desk and toward Cassie. "Thank you. Do I know you?"

"I'm not sure you do, but you know my grandmother, Dorothy Merrick. She was a friend of Norma's."

Helen nodded. "Oh, yes. She's a nice woman. She'd visit often."

"I was there when the house burned." Cassie

spoke softly. "I was knocked unconscious from the explosion. I wish I could have helped Norma."

"I heard someone else was there. That was you?" Helen frowned. "How awful."

"It was."

"And it was such a beautiful home," Lexy interjected. "You must have been heartbroken to lose that job, and even more sad when the house burned down."

For a moment, Helen's eyebrows twitched. "Well, yes. It was a lovely job. I was sorry to see Norma leave the house. But I looked forward to seeing her here at the Villa. We'd become quite close over the years." She stared off into the distance for a moment.

"She must have been fond of you, too, to leave you money in the will." Cassie moved her head into Helen's line of sight.

"What do you know about that?" Helen scrunched her face slightly.

"I know she took care of those she loved."

"Well, I wouldn't say ten thousand dollars will take care of me, but it was a nice gesture. I'm glad the Villa was eager to take me back as a full-time nurse."

"Ten thousand? That's all?" Cassie asked. "Did you know you were in the will?"

Helen furrowed her brows. "Uh, no. Why are you asking me?"

"Just curious."

She glanced at her watch. "I have to go. My shift is ending." She grabbed a stack of files from the counter. "Thank you for your condolences."

"Nice to meet you." Lexy waved.

Helen looked at Lexy but didn't reply. She turned and walked off.

"That was interesting," Cassie said. "What do you think?"

"I think there's something fishy about nurse Helen." Lexy put her hand on her hip.

"I agree."

"Didn't she say her shift was ending?"

Cassie nodded. "Let's see where she goes."

"Cool! A car chase." Lexy grinned as she followed Cassie down the hall to the front door.

Cassie laughed. "Somehow I don't think it will come to that."

"I can hope."

The girls signed out and stepped back outside. They walked down the now leaf-free sidewalk and headed to the parking lot.

"Do you really think Helen could be guilty of murdering Norma?" Lexy asked.

"I'm not sure. But someone is."

"Norma?" The scruffy-faced gardener looked up from a flower bed near the edge of the lot. He was adding mulched leaves to cover the plants before winter. "Are you talking about Norma

Clarkson?"

"Yes." Cassie stopped at the edge of the parking lot. "Why?"

"She was my boss." The gardener stood and slapped his gloves together to get rid of the caked-on dirt. "I did the gardening at the estate for the last year."

"Really." Cassie approached the man. "I'm Cassie. I was there when the explosion happened."

He took off his glove and shook her outstretched hand. "Carl. Carl North. Nice to meet you."

"And this is Lexy."

They exchanged greetings.

"Sorry, I didn't mean to eavesdrop." Carl fidgeted with the gloves. "But do you really think Helen was involved in the murder? I thought the son had been arrested."

"He has, but we know he didn't do it. And if *he* didn't, someone else did."

Carl scratched his chin. "It could be her, I suppose. She always behaved a bit strangely."

"What do you mean?" Cassie asked.

"I don't know how to explain it exactly. But I never trusted her. She had an air about her."

"I see. Anything else?"

Carl thought for a moment. "Actually, a bunch of stuff went missing as Norma was packing. I overheard her talking to Gretchen the housekeeper about it once while I worked on flowers by the front porch. She chalked it up to a bad memory, but I wouldn't be the least bit surprised if Helen was involved. She seems self-righteous to me, always acting like the world owes her or something."

"Interesting." Cassie glanced at Lexy, who darted her eyebrows up for a second. "Do you really think she'd be capable of murder?"

"Possibly." He shrugged. "She's not an overly warm person, if you know what I mean. And she's certainly a tough old broad."

"There she is, Cass." Lexy elbowed her friend in the side.

"Okay. Thank you very much, Mr. North. We appreciate your help."

"Anytime." He waved and put his gloves back on as he crouched over the flower bed again.

The girls jogged the short distance to Lexy's car and hopped in.

"Let's see where she goes." Lexy grinned.

"Remember. *Not* a car chase." Cassie fastened her seatbelt.

And it wasn't a car chase—at all. They followed Helen up the street into Banford, and into the parking lot of the grocery store. They sat anxiously waiting in their car until she came out with a bag of groceries. Cassie's eyes widened as Helen marched directly to Lexy's car and knocked on

Cassie's window.

Cassie tensed and put it down.

"Are you following me?" Helen sneered.

"We're getting groceries," Lexy called from the driver's seat.

"Sure, you are. What do you want from me?"

Cassie opened her mouth, but no words came out. What did they want? They wanted to catch a killer, and they thought it might be Helen. She couldn't very well say that, could she? "We have some... unanswered questions about Norma's death."

"Are you kidding me?" Helen screeched. "Are you suggesting I might be involved? For a measly ten grand?" She pointed her finger at Cassie. "Leave me alone, you hear? I've had a hard enough time losing Norma and adjusting to a new life."

"I'm sorry. We only—"

"Leave me alone, or I'll call the cops." Helen turned on her heel and stomped to her car.

"So..." Lexy shifted her eyes back and forth. "Does that make her a more likely suspect or less likely?"

"Good question." Cassie put her window back up. "Really good question."

Chapter 15

Cassie barely had her foot in the door to her building when Rick sent her a text.

"Come by the office when you get a chance."

Cassie checked the time. Almost four. She quickly sent him a "K." and headed back out the door. The real estate office was only a block and a half away from Cassie's building. She might as well head there now.

Moments later, she stepped through the door to Rick's office. He leaned over the reception desk, rummaging through a pile of papers. The chair was empty. Cassie was pretty sure the afternoon reception lady left at four.

"I'm here. What's up?"

Rick looked up from the mess he'd created.

"Hey! That was quick."

Cassie leaned against the wall and crossed her arms. "Lexy just dropped me off. We went to talk to Helen Gallagher at the Villa."

"Oh yeah?" He came around the desk and sat on the edge. "I have some news too."

"Really? You first."

"Nope. Let's hear yours first. Save the best for last." He smirked.

"Very funny." Cassie walked to the desk, sat in the empty reception chair, and put her foot on the edge of an open drawer. "She inherited ten thousand dollars in the will."

"Really?" Rick turned to face her and shimmied his backside to a more comfortable position on the desk. "Is that worth killing for?"

"I wouldn't think so, but she seemed rather distraught about the whole situation. Especially when we started asking questions."

"Maybe she's distraught over the death of her employer."

"Possibly, but she turned pretty defensive when we asked about it." Cassie put her foot on the floor and twirled the chair back and forth. "And not only that, we ran into Norma's gardener, outside."

"Carl?"

"Yeah. He seemed pretty convinced Helen wasn't an upright citizen. He thinks she's been stealing from Norma, and he doesn't doubt she could have pulled the whole thing off."

"Interesting." Rick tapped his chin. "But it doesn't feel right to me. Even if she was stealing, would she have set the explosion? And killed Norma? All for a measly ten thousand dollars? She would need more of a motive."

Cassie frowned. "I suppose you're right. But maybe she didn't know she was only getting ten grand. Maybe she thought it was more."

"Did she even know she was in the will in the first place?"

"No. At least she says she didn't."

"There you go. I think it's safe to say it isn't her."

Cassie sighed. She knew Rick was right. Not that she wanted Helen to be guilty, but she did want to solve this case and get it over with.

"Ready for my news?"

"Okay, big shot. Tell me yours."

"Guess who came in here asking if the Clarkson estate was still for sale?"

"Who?" Cassie crossed her arms in front of her.

"Harlan Waller."

"Harlan? The military guy? Why would he still be interested?"

"He claims he really liked the property, but the house was much too large for him. Now that it's gone, he wondered if the land was up for grabs."

"Hmm." Cassie propped her elbow on the

armrest and rested her chin on her hand. "That could be a motive. He wanted the land, so get rid of the house and buy the land cheaper?"

"That's what I thought. Until I talked to him some more."

"What do you mean?"

"When he named his price, it was well below what the land is worth, even without the house." Rick shrugged.

"But that doesn't make sense. Then why look at the full estate in the first place? It was priced *really* high."

"He said he was in the area looking at a lot for sale by a private seller. He drove by the open house and decided to check it out."

Cassie shook her head. "So why spend so much time in the basement? Something doesn't add up."

"I don't know. But he did say he'd wanted to come by the office earlier this week, as soon as he'd heard about the fire in the news, but he was away at a military training session in Toronto from Monday until this morning."

"Great, Rick. How is this supposed to be helpful?"

"It eliminates him as a suspect."

"And puts me right back down to none." She rubbed her face.

"You'll figure it out." He walked around the desk and lightly punched her arm. "I know you will."

"Nice. Thanks."

"Why don't you go for a walk or something? You always talk about how nature helps clear your head."

"Now *that's* a good idea." Cassie stood and gave Rick a quick hug. "I'll catch you later."

Cassie walked back up the street to her building. Rick was right. A walk would do her wonders right now. She could drive to the forest and take another look for the parula.

She jogged up the stairs to her apartment and grabbed her birding bag. It was heavy, so she removed the scope and set it on her counter. She wouldn't need it in the woods. Her binoculars, camera, and two bird books would be enough for today.

On the way out, she popped into Olde Crow Primitives to give Pumpkin a head scratch and to let Maggie know her birding plans. Grams had headed home for the day, so Maggie would close the shop by herself and return Pumpkin to the apartment.

Within a half hour, she walked on the trail, breathing in the cool autumn air and feeling the cushion of orange pine needles beneath her feet.

She already felt better.

A couple of blue jays piped up to announce her arrival, followed by a murder of three crows coming in to take a peek. They too, signalled her presence with a few loud calls.

Ahead, a squirrel joined the choir and chattered at Cassie until she passed by. She frowned. If the parula was still in the area, it had plenty of time to hide before she reached its part of the woods.

Even so, nature's chorus soothed her mind as she tried to piece together the puzzle surrounding the explosion and Norma's death. She couldn't completely rule out Helen Gallagher. It's possible she had another motive Cassie had yet to discover. And in Harlan Waller's case, it was only his word that gave him an alibi. But Cassie knew it was pretty safe to say neither of them were involved.

Even though she couldn't make sense of the case, she was grateful for the break from thinking about Daniel and Spencer.

She entered the part of the forest where the Bird Club saw the parula. A couple of chickadees fluttered through the trees for a few minutes, but other than that, there was no activity. The woods were silent here, and for the entire half hour she slowly and quietly paced the section of path, binoculars in hand. She was patient, but to no avail.

Finally giving up, she headed back down the trail to her SUV. The last portion of trail passed along the edge of a grassy meadow, and as Cassie emerged from the forest and made her way alongside the field, a flicker of white and black drew her attention.

She quickly raised her binoculars to her eyes and smiled as she spotted a small flock of snow buntings. Whereas the northern parula was late in heading south, these buntings were a bit early arriving here. This is where they spent their winter, as their summer habitat was north in the Arctic. Cassie smiled. She'd seen plenty of buntings flitting around, landing, and then rising into the air. Landing and rising again.

A brown blur caught her eye. She carefully observed the dancing flock until they settled down on the ground. That's when she saw it.

A Lapland longspur!

She suppressed a squeal as the brown-and-white bird foraged along the ground with the buntings. This was a lifer for her. She knew they often flew with buntings and horned larks, but she'd never seen one. How many times had she stopped to watch a flock of buntings in the winter, hoping to see a longspur? And now, there was one right in front of her.

She whispered thanks to the Lord while she continued to enjoy the bird's beauty, standing on the spot until long after the flock of buntings and the longspur flew away.

After a few more breaths of fresh air, Cassie walked to her SUV and leaned against the side, overlooking the meadow. Her stomach churned.

Yes, it was lovely to see the longspur, but now it was back to reality. And the reality was, her life outside of birdwatching was a complete mess.

Rick's friend Wesley sat in jail. She had no real suspects, and no clue where to look next.

And of course, there was the Daniel and Spencer drama.

Had accepting the date with Spencer ruined her friendship with Daniel? Would things ever be the same with him?

And was she horrible for not talking to Spencer about Daniel? Was she leading Spencer on?

Or worse yet, did she *want* to lead him on? Was it possible she was actually interested in the hot firefighter who loved Jesus?

Cassie climbed into the vehicle, her head spinning. She felt like she was living in a soap opera, and all she wanted was for someone to turn off the television.

Chapter 16

Not only did Hardcastle Restaurant and Pub make the great breakfasts Grams and Cassie enjoyed on Sunday mornings, they also had great takeout. And takeout was just what Cassie needed after a day like today.

She parked her SUV in her usual spot behind her building, strapped her birding bag over her shoulder, then grabbed her purse and bottled drink with one hand and the takeout container with the other. She managed to slam the car door with her foot and, on her way to the side entry door to the building, trod past The Book Nook window, resolved not to look in.

At the side entry, she stared at the locked door in front of her. Apparently she hadn't thought this through too well. She balanced the drink on the takeout while she pressed her purse against her leg and rummaged through it with her semi-free hand.

A jingling sound came from the bottom of her bag. The keys were in there, somewhere. After a bit more fumbling, she pulled them out, but before she could find the right key, the door swung toward her. She quickly inched backward, and the drink flew off of the takeout container.

"I got it!" Daniel snatched it out of the air before it hit the ground.

"Uh, thanks." Cassie tossed her keys back into her purse, slipped the strap over the backpack on her shoulder, and grabbed the drink. As she did so, the purse slid, and the strap landed on the crook of her elbow.

"Let me help." Daniel grabbed the takeout and the drink, so Cassie could adjust her backpack and purse. He continued to lean against the door to hold it open for her.

Cassie squeezed by him into the hallway. His smell of leather and old books was stronger than the chicken Caesar salad and fries in her takeout container.

"I can bring these up for you." Daniel pointed his head toward the stairs.

"I think I can manage, now that I'm through the locked door." She grabbed the container and brushed his hand in the process. The familiar electricity surged through her and made her heart beat faster. Cassie hesitated, and they both held the container for a moment. His gaze locked on hers, and she couldn't look away.

She'd missed him over the past few days—the electricity, the way his eyes seemed to stare into her soul, and his company. She missed their daily conversations and the laughter.

He let go of the container, and the softness in his eyes abruptly faded. It was almost as if they had turned a shade darker. "How was your date?"

Cassie gulped. "Oh, uh. Fine, I guess."

"Just fine?"

"Yes. Just fine." She grabbed the drink and turned to go up the stairs.

"Where did he take you?"

Cassie went up two stairs and turned around. "Do you really want to do this?"

"No. Not really."

She went up the third and fourth steps.

"I don't trust the guy," he called after her.

Fifth step. Sixth step. "That's nice. Do you trust me?"

Daniel darted after her. "What's that supposed to mean?"

She reached the first midway landing and turned to face him again. "Do you trust my judgement? Or don't you?"

"Frankly, I don't see how that has anything to do with Spencer."

"It has everything to do with him. If he was some kind of freak, don't you think I would sense that?"

"Maybe. Maybe not." He reached the landing and rubbed the back of his neck.

Cassie stared at Daniel. What was the point of this conversation? "You're just jealous."

"Maybe I am!"

Not the answer she expected. She headed up the next set of stairs. "But you and I... we're just friends." Here they were, going around the same familiar circle.

"Not this again. Don't deny it Cassie. We've been more than friends for a while." Daniel followed close behind.

"But we can't be."

"Oh, that's right. I don't measure up to your standards."

She stopped abruptly as she reached the landing for her floor. Her purse fell off of her shoulder again and pulled her arm. "That's not true!"

"Isn't it? Why won't you date me? Say it."

Cassie stretched out her arm until the purse slid the rest of the way down and hit the floor. She continued to hold the drink in her hand and balance the takeout container in the other.

"You know why."

"Say it."

She felt tears well up in her eyes. "Because you aren't a Christian. You can't be the spiritual leader of the relationship I need you to be."

"I didn't think anyone could live up to your expectations, and that in time you would come around." He bent down to grab her purse. "But I guess I was wrong." He thrust her purse at her, and she wrapped her arm around it to hold it in place.

"Daniel..."

"Looks like you've found someone who does." He nodded toward her apartment door.

"What?" She turned. An Old Log Cabin whiskey bottle sat on the floor at her apartment door with a single red rose in it.

Daniel headed back down the stairs.

"Wait," Cassie muttered softly, the word resonating the doubt she felt in saying it.

"Goodbye, Cassie." Daniel took the rest of the stairs two by two and disappeared into the hallway below within moments. She heard the bookstore door open and shut.

What did he mean? Goodbye for now? Goodbye forever?

The hallway was now as empty as she felt.

Cassie shuffled to the apartment door and looked at the whiskey bottle and the rose. It was a sweet gesture. There was no denying it.

She opened the door with her full hands, thankful she didn't lock it most days, and entered the apartment.

"Rowr!" Pumpkin immediately greeted her by rubbing against Cassie's leg, effectively causing her to stumble. The purse and the bottled drink flew out of her hand, but she managed to catch herself before she dumped the takeout.

"Silly cat," she cooed. "I missed you too." She quickly put the takeout on the counter, whipped the birding bag off her shoulder, and picked up Pumpkin to cradle her.

The cat purred loudly. Cassie drank in its soothing effect.

After a few deep breaths, she put the cat down, picked up the drink and her purse, and retrieved the whiskey bottle from outside the door. She'd have to call Spencer to thank him, but she didn't think she could handle it quite yet.

Cassie pulled a plate out of the cupboard and opened the takeout container. The aroma of the chicken Caesar salad and fries wafted out of the box, but her stomach no longer felt excited about the food. She dumped it on the plate anyway and decided to pick away at it to at least get something into her.

She put the pop bottle into the fridge, deciding not to tempt fate and open the shaken drink tonight. A bottle of water would do just fine for now.

Cassie plopped down on the couch with her plate and pulled an afghan over her legs. Pumpkin wasted no time in curling up beside her and pawing at her lap for her share of the chicken. Cassie obliged.

After forcing a few bites down, Cassie brought her plate to the kitchen, boxed the rest of the meal back into the takeout container, and stuck it in the fridge. Then she returned to the couch and curled up with the afghan and her faithful feline.

Her head was such a mess. Between the murder, and the suspects, and Spencer, and Daniel, a hurricane whirled in her mind.

Her heart hurt. The tears flowed, but it felt good to release them. "Oh, God. Please help me figure things out." Cassie wiped her face with a corner of the afghan. "But I guess that's the problem, isn't it? I've been trying to figure things out on my own again. Forgive me, Lord."

Pumpkin looked at Cassie with wide eyes and pawed at her arm. Then she jumped directly into her lap and curled into a ball—a large ball, but a ball nonetheless.

"I don't know who murdered Norma. But you do. Please show me the truth so I can help Wesley." She suddenly felt lighter.

"And I really don't know what to do about Spencer and Daniel. But again, You do." Cassie sniffed. "You know who is right for me. I trust You to show me who it is."

She waited a moment, looking to the ceiling and waiting for a voice.

And then it hit her.

Wait.

God had told her to wait. To be patient. Just like she had been when trying to catch a glimpse of the northern parula, and in waiting, the Lapland longspur came along and surprised her.

Was it a message?

Maybe it *wasn't* Daniel God had been telling her to wait for. Maybe she needed to wait, because there was someone *else* He had in mind for her. Cassie continued to mull this thought over in her mind.

Could it be? Maybe God had wanted her to wait because He planned to bring Spencer into her life.

Spencer? She tried to picture herself with him, as a couple, but the image wouldn't quite form in her mind.

He wasn't part of her plan, but she quickly reminded herself *her* plans were not always God's plans. She needed to trust God.

Spencer was kind, loving, devoted to helping others, and above all, he loved God. And he was pretty nice to look at too. Heat rose to her cheeks, even though no one was around to see her.

But then there was Daniel. He was also kind,

loving, and helpful. And there was something else—he was passionate. About life, about his photography, and about her. And although he might not be as muscular as Spencer, he could definitely hold his own in the looks department. Her heart beat faster just thinking about him.

But Daniel didn't love God. Not in the way he needed to for her to be united with him, anyway.

Cassie sighed. Spencer was certainly a great catch.

But he wasn't Daniel.

She looked upward. "Is it Spencer? Is he why you wanted me to wait?" She listened for the still small voice.

When she heard none, she continued, "Or do you want me to wait longer for Daniel?"

Silence.

"Please tell me, God. Tell me what to do."

More silence.

Cassie turned to look at the whiskey bottle with the rose. It was so sweet of Spencer to leave it for her. She smiled.

Then she thought of Daniel, and her stomach tied up in knots.

Ugh. That was it. If she was going to go by what felt more peaceful, then she'd just made her decision.

She reached for her phone to give Spencer a call and thank him for the lovely gift.

Chapter 17

Smash!

Cassie jolted upright in bed to the sound of breaking glass. The red numbers on her alarm clock glowed two-something.

She quickly swung her legs over the side and rubbed her eyes. Pumpkin meowed her disapproval from her spot on the end of the bed.

The sound had come from downstairs.

Cassie gave her head a shake to wake herself, and the reality of the situation hit her.

Someone was downstairs! A rush of adrenaline gave her the energy she needed to run out to the kitchen and grab her store keys.

Wait. Her phone. She ran to the bedroom to get it in case she needed a flashlight or a way to call for help.

Cassie opened her apartment door and squinted as she stepped into the well-lit hallway. Not waiting for her eyes to adjust, she darted to the stairs.

A noise on the stairwell above caught her attention. She gasped as a figure moved down the stairs toward her.

Daniel.

"Are you all right?" He ran his hands through his hair, the muscles bulging in his bicep as he did so. He wore plaid pajama pants and a sleeveless white undershirt. "I heard a window break."

She gulped. Now was not the time to notice how hot Daniel was. "I'm fine. I was just heading downstairs to see what was going on."

"I'll go with you." He passed her and went first, moving cautiously and quietly.

At the shop entry, Daniel put his finger to his lips and his ear against the door. After a moment, he turned and whispered, "It seems quiet."

Cassie carefully slipped the key into the lock and turned it.

Daniel led the way and slowly opened the door. Light from the hallway cast shadows behind the tall display shelves. He fumbled around on the wall, trying to find the light switch.

Thump.

Something at the front of the store made a

noise. Cassie jumped and unexpectedly found herself wrapped in the safety of Daniel's embrace. He'd turned so he was between her and the noise. He held her tightly, protecting her with his strong arms. She couldn't deny how natural it felt.

Trying to keep her wits about her, Cassie pulled out of the protective hug and found the light switch on the wall.

The rack directly in front of them displayed long wooden signs. Daniel grabbed one and held it like a bat. "Is anyone there?"

Cassie gasped and covered her mouth. One of the tall windows at the side of her store had been smashed. She pointed it out to Daniel.

He had his eyes set toward the front of the store but kept one hand on Cassie's arm, keeping her safely behind him. "We're calling the police. Come out now!"

Cassie took his cue and dialed 911.

"Watch it!" He stopped her. Glass covered the floor in front of him, and they were both in bare feet. Daniel quickly checked around the remaining shelves and behind the cash counter.

The dispatcher came on the line. Cassie filled her in on the details. The operator promised to send a policeman out immediately.

"All clear." Daniel returned and lowered the sign weapon. "It doesn't look like anyone is inside."

Cassie groaned and stepped carefully into the

next aisle. An old red brick sat on the floor in the midst of the broken glass. "Oh, that's just great."

"Don't touch it." Daniel grabbed her hand. "There could be fingerprints on it."

Cassie knew that already, but decided not to mention it. She did, however, want to examine it.

"Ouch!" She hoisted her foot into the air. Blood dripped onto the wooden floor.

"Cassie!" Daniel whisked her into his arms and carried her across the store. She had no choice but to wrap her arm around his neck and hang on. He gently set her on the cash counter and grabbed her leg. "Let me see."

"It's only a little cut." She tried to wriggle her foot out of his grasp, but pain shot up her leg. "Ah!"

"There's a piece of glass stuck in there. Hang on." He carefully pulled on the shard of glass. "There. I think I got it all."

"Thank you." The autumn air had filled the shop, and she rubbed her bare arms with her hands to create warmth. She suddenly looked down and realized she was wearing her sleeveless nightie that hung only mid-thigh. Heat instantly rose to her cheeks.

"Stay there." Daniel went for the first aid kit, hanging on the wall behind the cash.

And what about her hair? She felt her head. Ugh! She'd put it in a ponytail before bed, but her hair currently stuck out of it on all sides. She quickly pulled the elastic out and smoothed her curls. She settled for a messy bun.

Daniel returned and propped open the kit on the counter beside her. He rummaged through it and took out an antibiotic ointment and a bandage. As he worked on her foot, the sides of his jaw pulsed, and the veins popped out a bit in his temples.

"There. Good as new." He shut the kit and looked at Cassie.

There was something new in his eyes. A longing, mixed with sorrow.

"Thank you." She gulped.

He gently put his hands around her and lifted her down. She could have a thousand shards of glass in her feet and wouldn't feel them over the strength of the electricity running through her body.

When he set her down, he didn't let go. "You're cold." He drew her into a tight hug. "I'm so glad you're safe. When I heard the breaking glass, I…"

"Daniel…"

He pulled back a bit and gently lifted her chin. "I'm sorry I've been such a jerk. You're right. I have been jealous. I don't want to lose you."

His blue eyes were looking into her soul again. She gulped.

"You mean the world to me, Cassie Bridgestone. I don't know what I'd do without you."

Tears welled in his eyes, and one eventually slipped out. Cassie wiped it from his cheek. They stood there, hands on one another's faces for a moment. Time stood still.

And then Daniel leaned in, his lips parted, and Cassie closed her eyes.

Whoop!

A police siren outside the front door jolted them apart before their lips could touch. The red and blue lights flashed through the windows.

Officer Welby had arrived.

And not a moment too soon.

Daniel grabbed a blanket from one of the store shelves and wrapped it around Cassie. She pulled it tight to cover her nightie.

Moments later, Officer Welby stood on the broken glass with his big, shiny police boots. "Looks like a standard act of vandalism to me." He finished writing in his little coil notebook and swung it shut. "I'll write it up in the morning."

"That's it?" Cassie huffed. "You're not going to do anything?"

"Nothing to do. Unfortunately, there are no security cameras in the village, so there's no way to know who did it."

"What about getting fingerprints from the brick?"

Officer Welby shrugged. "No point. No one

would be stupid enough to leave prints on it."

Cassie frowned. He could at least pretend he was making an effort.

"I'll be off then."

"Wait." She held up her hand. "I have a theory."

"What do you mean?" Daniel turned to Cassie and raised his eyebrows.

"Norma's murderer did it. I'm getting close to catching him. Or her."

Officer Welby laughed. "This isn't *Murder She Wrote*. Wesley Clarkson is the murderer, and he's already in jail, Miss Bridgestone." Officer Welby shifted his weight to one foot. More glass crunched under his boot.

"Except he didn't do it." She put her hand on her hip. "There are plenty of others with motives and means."

"Oh, really." His smug look made Cassie want to slap him. "Tell me then, Nancy Drew."

"Don't you mean Jessica Fletcher?" She sassed him right back.

"Why don't we sit over here and talk this through?" Daniel put his hand on the small of Cassie's back and led her to the stools behind the cash counter. She took a seat, but Officer Welby remained standing on the other side.

Cassie spent the next few minutes telling him about Harlan Waller, Helen Gallagher, and the suspicions she had about both.

Officer Welby yawned. "It's late, Miss Bridgestone. I suggest you go back to bed and finish this fictional dream of yours before the sun rises."

"You won't even look into them?" Cassie shook her head in disbelief.

"I think you seem to forget I'm a trained investigator. I've solved dozens of big-city crimes—all without your help, I might add."

"You certainly didn't get very far without my help this summer." She narrowed her eyes and crossed her arms in front of her.

He met her gaze with narrowed eyes of his own. "*Helping* with one or two crimes doesn't make you an expert."

"Maybe it *is* time to get back to bed." Daniel lightly pushed on Cassie's back to make her hop off the stool.

"I'll file the *vandalism* report in the morning. In the meantime, I suggest you get this cleaned up. It looks like it might rain." He threw another smug smile her way. "I'll let myself out."

The door slammed shut behind him.

"Ugh!" Cassie threw her arms up, letting the blanket fall to the floor. "That man infuriates me!"

"Why don't you run upstairs and put something warmer on. I'll start cleaning."

She didn't feel very cold at the moment, but she decided to take Daniel's suggestion. By the time she returned, wearing yoga pants and a long-sleeved plaid shirt that hung almost as low as her nightie had, Daniel had already swept up most of the debris.

She grabbed a rag from the cleaning closet and began to remove glass shards from the shelving displays.

They spent the next few hours working and chatting like they did before the whole fire and Spencer thing had happened. At seven, Daniel ran upstairs to get his wallet and headed to get them breakfast from Drummond's Bakery. Cassie watched his athletic form dart around a car as he jogged across the street. She was so grateful for his help, and she took comfort in the fact he was talking to her like normal.

Except it wasn't normal.

Not after the way he'd almost kissed her.

Her heart sank. Where would things go from here? Would he continue on in a friendship with her? Or would he expect more?

And if she chose to date Spencer, would Daniel completely disappear from her life and become only a tenant she sometimes crossed paths with in the stairwell?

The thought turned her stomach.

Nothing seemed to be the right answer.

She shook the thoughts from her head and stared at the red brick sitting on the cash counter.

Anger seeped in where confusion had just been. Who dared to smash her store window with a brick? It was a cheap, low act of cowardice.

Was it intended as a warning? Cassie firmly believed what she had told Officer Welby. Someone didn't like her poking around in the murder investigation.

Tough. Now, more than ever, she was determined to find the killer.

Chapter 18

Thankfully, Grams had eagerly agreed to come in for an extra shift Saturday so Cassie could catch up on some sleep. Daniel had boarded up the broken window in Olde Crow Primitives, and Cassie had already called insurance to put in a claim.

With that taken care of, Pumpkin nestled at the foot of the bed on a comfy quilt, and Cassie climbed into bed well after the sun rose, feeling like she could sleep for days.

Still, sleep eluded her.

Her mind jumped from Daniel to Spencer, from the murder to Wesley, and from Harlan to Helen. After tossing and turning and begging God to quiet her mind, she eventually fell asleep.

She woke at ten with a sudden and clear plan. After a quick shower and a couple of short phone calls, Cassie jogged down the stairs to meet Lexy in the parking lot at ten thirty.

It was the perfect day to head to the Clarkson estate and snoop around. Mystery shows and books had taught her it was always good to return to the scene of the crime and take a second look.

After the short drive, Cassie and Lexy ducked under the caution tape and walked around the rubble and burnt remains of Norma's home.

"This is so sad." Lexy frowned, picking up a charred picture frame with no painting left.

Cassie agreed. She hadn't been prepared for the effect walking through someone's burned belongings would have on her. Especially since that person died here.

They explored the rubble a while longer and met in front of the gaping hole where the investigators had cleared the way to examine the source of the explosion in the basement.

"Should we go down there?" Lexy grimaced.

"I don't know. It doesn't look safe, and I'm pretty sure the fire marshal thoroughly examined the area, anyway." Cassie crouched and stared into the hole a bit longer. "That's strange. Why would the murderer start the explosion against the wall of the cellar?"

"What do you mean?"

"If you wanted to topple a house, wouldn't you put the explosion near the middle to reach all sides equally?"

"I don't know." Lexy studied the explosion site. "Maybe blowing out a wall has a greater effect."

"You could be right." Cassie shrugged and stood. "Let's look around the grounds a bit."

Lexy wiped the soot from her hands onto her jeans and nodded.

They jumped off the rubble and crossed back under the caution tape. Together, they roamed the front yard and then the back, kicking their feet through the fallen leaves as they walked.

The shrubs and landscaping surrounding the house were either lying under the remains, burnt, or dead from the close vicinity to the heat of the fire. The outer perimeter of the estate, however, was still as pristine as the first day she saw it.

"What are the ugly dirt spots?" Lexy pointed to the various refilled holes on the lawn.

"Norma had the gardener dig up a number of trees and plants before she listed the house. For friends or something."

"That's unusual, isn't it?"

Cassie shrugged. "To each his own, I guess." But as she studied the locations, she *did* think it odd trees had previously been in those places. They seemed spaced so... randomly, and some were filled unevenly. "Watch your step. It's possible there are more under these leaves."

Lexy nodded and trod carefully.

A large detached storage shed on the far side of the property caught her eye. "Let's check it out."

The girls crossed the yard and the driveway. Cassie kicked away a pile of soggy leaves that had collected in front of the door and pulled on the handle. "It's open."

"Wow!" Lexy's eyes widened. "What is all this stuff?"

Enough daylight shone through the dirty, old windows to reveal dozens of boxes and totes stacked on top of each other, creating a maze through the interior of the building, which by the looks of the high ceilings and a sealed door on the side, used to be a carriage house. Cassie popped open the lid of a blue tote and drew out a flowered teacup. "There's an antique set of dishes in here."

Lexy peeked in another tote on top of a stack. "And a couple of old quilts in this one."

"This must be all of the stuff Norma was getting rid of before she moved."

"Should we be looking through it then?" Lexy frowned. "It seems kind of... invasive."

"I don't know. We need clues, but I agree. It doesn't feel right. Let's see what's farther back."

The girls pushed their way around boxes and piles. The deeper they went into the building, the older the boxes became. Eventually, they stood among wooden crates filled with old tools, flower pots, transistor radio parts, and newspapers.

"Hey." Cassie reached into a crate and pulled out a bottle. "This is just like the bottle Spencer bought for me." She peered into the crate. "There's a bunch of them in here."

"Spencer bought you a whiskey bottle?" Lexy chuckled.

"Oh. Yeah." Cassie felt her cheeks warm as she returned the bottle to the crate. "When we toured Mrs. Dingham's Antiques, I mentioned I liked it. I found it at my apartment door yesterday with a rose in it."

Lexy put her hand on her chest. "Aw! That's so sweet!"

Cassie shrugged one shoulder and smiled.

"Really?" Lexy raised her eyebrows. "You've got nothing to say about it?"

"What do you want me to say?"

"How wonderful it is to have *two* gorgeous guys beating down your door."

"I wish it was wonderful, but it's not. I've never felt more confused in my life." She dropped her shoulders and closed her eyes. "Daniel almost kissed me last night."

"What?" Lexy's eyes grew as big as the saucers in the dish set Cassie had found. "And you're only telling me *now*?"

"Officer Welby arrived and interrupted the moment."

Lexy rolled her eyes. "Figures."

"That's a good thing. I can't kiss Daniel!"

"Why not?"

Cassie rubbed her face with her hands. "Because we're just friends! Why does no one understand that?"

"Everyone sees quite clearly what is going on. *You're* the one who needs to see that you're *not* just friends." She smirked.

"What? Why is that funny?"

Lexy pointed at Cassie's face. "You kinda smeared soot on your cheeks."

"Ugh!" Cassie looked at her dirty hands then opted to use her sweater sleeve to wipe her face. "Do I have it all?"

"Yes." Lexy still smirked.

"Very funny. Can we look for more clues, please?"

Lexy scanned the room. "These antiques are bound to be worth a lot of money."

"I bet they are."

"Do you think these would have anything to do with the murder?"

Cassie shook her head. "I don't see how. Even if there's thousands of dollars' worth of stuff here, it doesn't compare to the value of the estate or the insurance policy." She sighed and plucked some cobwebs out of her hair. "Let's head back to town and get cleaned up."

The girls weaved their way out of the shed and

closed the door like they had found it. Cassie drove back to her building, dropped Lexy at her car, and headed up to her apartment to take yet another shower.

She put on a pajama short and tank top set and covered it with her fuzzy, knee-length bathrobe, not caring that it was one o'clock but feeling even more grateful to Grams for taking her shift today.

Cassie plopped onto the sofa beside Pumpkin with a big mug of Earl Grey tea in hand. The cat heaved herself closer and settled with her two front paws on Cassie's lap. She had meant to drop Pumpkin off at the shop with Grams and Maggie before she went to the estate, but now she was glad she'd forgotten. She could use the comfort.

"What do I do, Pumpkin roll?" She stroked her cat. Wesley was going to be transferred to a real prison soon, and he'd sit there for months while he waited for a trial where he'd likely be convicted. Early this morning, she'd felt great about everything. Someone was worried enough to throw a brick through her store window. But in reality, all she had were a couple of unlikely suspects.

She frowned. Maybe Officer Welby was right. Maybe it was a random act of vandalism, and maybe she was making a fool of herself looking into the case.

Yet, Wesley was innocent, wasn't he? Then

someone else *had* to have done it.

But who? And where did she go from here?

It all seemed so hopeless.

Cassie sighed and took a long sip of her tea. Her stomach turned. The truth was, Wesley's life hung in the balance, and she wasn't near as worried about helping him as she was about what was going on with Daniel and Spencer. What kind of person did that make her? What kind of *Christian* was she?

And therein lay the problem. All this time she had been keeping Daniel at arm's length because he didn't share her faith. All this time, she'd held back and insisted they just be friends.

But Lexy, like everyone else, was right.

She'd led him on.

There was no way their relationship was only a friendship, no matter how loudly she screamed it from the rooftops to convince herself. As much as she'd claimed she was opposed to him trying to kiss her last night, or this morning, or whenever it was, she had to admit she was very sad they were interrupted.

Cassie had *wanted* the kiss to happen.

She longed for it.

And that was a problem. She'd been a fool. The last few months she'd been kidding herself about having only a friendship with him. There were definite feelings in her heart for Daniel.

Deep feelings.

And she'd allowed them to grow, in spite of God's warning to her to wait. And now things were a mess. As much as it hurt her, she could not—no, *would* not, move into a relationship with Daniel unless he shared her faith. God had to remain most important in her life, and in any future marriage. She'd made a promise to Grams, and to God, and she intended to keep it.

It was her fault she'd let things go this far, and now she had to reap the consequences. No matter how painful.

Pumpkin kneaded Cassie's lap, and a claw poked through the bathrobe into Cassie's leg. She winced.

Even the cat knew it.

But she hated what the consequences of her disobedience would do to Daniel. What *she* had done to Daniel. She hoped he would forgive her, but she doubted he ever would.

A tear slipped down her cheek. She hoped she could forgive herself too.

A knock on the door brought her back to reality. Pumpkin jumped off the couch and hid under the coffee table. Cassie set down her tea and wiped the tear from her face.

She glanced at the clock on the wall. Almost one thirty. Did Lexy come back to hang out? The company would be nice.

The knock repeated as Cassie pulled the door open.

"Hey." Spencer had one very muscular arm above his head, leaning on the doorframe. "I heard at the station what happened here last night. Are you okay?"

Cassie nodded but couldn't stop the tears from filling her eyes and overflowing the sides.

"Cassie..." He used his thumb to gently wipe a tear from her cheek and held the side of her face.

When she didn't say anything, he pulled her into his arms.

She cried on his shoulder.

Chapter 19

At Spencer's insistence, Cassie sat on the couch while he made her a cup of tea. She pulled her fuzzy bathrobe tightly around her and snuggled into the warmth of it while Pumpkin jumped up beside her and curled into a ball on the afghan.

"Here you go." Spencer handed her the hot mug and sat down facing her on the sofa.

"Thank you." She held the mug in both hands and breathed in the soothing bergamot aroma of the Earl Grey.

Spencer tucked a curl behind her ear. Daniel often did the same thing, especially if she needed comfort. But he wasn't here right now. Spencer was.

"Do you want to talk about it?" His gruff voice

was low and full of concern.

Cassie shrugged. Talk about what? Daniel? To Spencer? Definitely not. But she could talk about the investigation. Maybe that would help. "I don't know what else to do to help Wesley."

"You must be close to something, if someone threw a brick through your window."

"Officer Welby insists it was an act of vandalism." Cassie frowned.

"Is that what you think?"

"I don't know. I didn't at first, but now I'm not sure."

"I think you *do* know. Tell me everything you've found out so far. Maybe it will make something click."

She took a sip of her tea. What had she found out? "There's not much to tell, unfortunately. Wesley is the prime suspect because of the house insurance policy and inheritance from his mother's will. He has no solid alibi, and he had TNT residue in his car trunk."

"Nothing changed there. You're sure he didn't do it?"

"Positive."

"Okay, who else is there?"

"I looked into the people who attended the open house. I combed through the list, and only two stood out as possibilities. The first was a guy who works at the quarry. His name is Jarvis. He gave me a hard time about signing in and showing his identification, but Harlan—he's the other suspect—coaxed him to follow the rules. Lexy and I figured since Jarvis worked at the quarry, he'd have access to explosives. But it turned out he didn't, and he was working at the time of the explosion."

Spencer nodded. "What about the other guy?"

"Harlan is in the military. He spent an unusual amount of time in the cellar, and has also visited Rick since the house burned down to inquire about purchasing the land. But he didn't offer enough money, and it seems he was out of town on Tuesday. Although I can't prove it."

"And if he really wanted the land, he would've offered more money to ensure he got it."

"Right." Cassie nodded.

"Anyone else?"

"Norma's nurse. Helen Gallagher. With Norma moving to the retirement villa, Helen was out of a job and had to find a new place to live. She also stood to inherit ten thousand dollars in the will." Cassie sipped her tea.

"She sounds like a reasonable suspect."

"I thought so. And supposedly she stole things from Norma. She was also pretty defensive when I talked to her about the will."

Spencer ran his hands through his hair. "But you don't think she did it?"

"She's strange, but no. I don't think she's a killer. She claims she never knew about the ten thousand, and she seemed legitimately broken up over Norma's death. She also sounded happy to be working at the villa, so she'd still see Norma. And ten thousand dollars doesn't seem like enough to kill someone for."

"Maybe she thought she'd inherit more?"

"Maybe." Cassie pressed her lips together.

"Okay." Spencer placed his arm across the back of the couch and lifted one leg onto the cushion in front of him. "Who else?"

Cassie shrugged. "That's it."

Spencer sighed. "No other clues?"

"Nope."

He put his hand on her shoulder. "It's okay. It'll come to you. If there's one thing I've figured out about you, it's that you're a smart girl. Really smart." He moved his hand and touched her cheek. "If anyone can get to the bottom of this, it's you."

Cassie reached up and clutched his hand, holding it against her face. "Thank you." She stared into his green eyes. They sparkled as he smiled.

"Anytime." He winked.

She lowered her hand, taking his with it, and held it in her lap. "Lexy and I went to the estate this morning to look around, but other than a shed full of antiques, we didn't find anything."

"Antiques?" Spencer raised his eyebrows and

smiled.

Cassie laughed. "Yes. I think it was mostly stuff Norma decided to get rid of as she downsized."

"Anything interesting? Old records perhaps?"

"Not that I noticed, but we didn't go through all the boxes." The whiskey bottle with the rose on the coffee table in front of her caught Cassie's eye. She stretched forward and grabbed it. "But there was a box of bottles like these."

"Really? Let me see that." Spencer took the bottle from her hand. He looked it over, held it up to check the bottom, and stared at the label. A corner was loose. "It looks like there's something else under here."

"Can you peel it off?"

"It might rip."

"That's okay. I know where I can get more." Cassie smirked.

"All right." He took the rose out and gently laid it on the table, hanging the wet stem off the edge. Pumpkin reached out her paw to swat the end of it. "Hey, Turkey. Leave that alone." He moved it out of her reach.

Cassie chuckled.

Spencer slowly plucked at the label. It was dry and crisp, and almost popped off in one piece. "Look." He held the bottle out to her.

A faded label underneath was still readable enough to make out the words "Canadian Club."

Another whiskey brand.

Cassie furrowed her brows. "Well, that's interesting." She jumped up and went to her office to retrieve her laptop. By the time she returned, Pumpkin had cuddled beside Spencer. "Traitor," she whispered as she sat back down.

Spencer laughed and scratched the cat under her chin.

"Let's see what we can find." Cassie typed, "Old Log Cabin whiskey Canadian Club" into the search bar. A list of results filled the computer screen, all with one name in common.

"By the look on your face, I take it you found something?" Spencer leaned in close beside her and looked at the screen. "What? Al Capone!"

Cassie forced a slow nod. "Old Log Cabin Whiskey was his brand. Look." She pointed at the screen. "So much Canadian liquor crossed the border through Detroit that he wanted a piece of the profit. He took Canadian Club whiskey and relabelled it under his own brand."

"Wow!" Spencer examined the bottle again. "This was Al Capone's?"

Cassie read some more. "Looks like it. And listen to this! Apparently, Bugs Moran was part of the partnership, but then began buying from hijackers and selling an inferior brand to make more money on his own. When that didn't work out, he started hijacking Al Capone's trucks. It's what led to the St. Valentine's Day Massacre!"

Spencer's mouth dropped open. "Woah. That's some heavy stuff." He looked at the bottle again, suddenly holding it a bit more gingerly. "You said there was a whole box of these bottles at the estate? Here in Banford?"

"There *are* rumours he was in this area. There's that old stone house in Kemptville." Cassie typed more into her laptop. "And the golf course he supposedly helped design to favour his left-hand swing."

"Now that you mention it, that does sound familiar. How much are the bottles worth?"

More typing. "Not much. Looks like around twenty-five dollars if they're empty."

"So the bottles themselves can't be a motive." Spencer rubbed the five o'clock shadow on his jaw.

Cassie's eyes widened.

"What?" Spencer asked.

"Hang on." She frantically typed another search into the computer. Then another, and another.

Spencer stared at the screen. "Well, would you look at that!"

Cassie turned to face him and couldn't help grinning like a young girl in a candy store. "That would explain the explosion."

Spencer put his hand on her cheek again. "I knew you'd figure it out."

"Only because you helped." She smiled,

enjoying his touch more than she thought she would.

He stared into her eyes a moment longer, caressing her cheek with his thumb.

Cassie held his gaze, unsure how to handle the sudden stirring in her heart.

Spencer leaned in and gently touched his lips to hers. She held her breath and closed her eyes, enjoying the softness and warmth of his lips. He moved his hand around to the back of her head, intertwining his fingers with her messy curls, and pulled her closer.

Her heart pounded.

And then Spencer pulled away. He sat back, caressed her cheek again, and smiled at her. "You're amazing. I wish I could stay and help you, but I have a shift at the fire station."

Cassie smiled. "You helped me a lot."

He winked at her as he stood. Pumpkin meowed and clawed at his leg. "Sorry kitty. I have to go to work."

Cassie laughed and followed Spencer to the door. She tugged the straps on her bathrobe to tighten it.

Spencer slipped his shoes onto his feet and pulled the door open. He turned back to her. "I'm really glad I stopped by today."

"Me too."

"C'mere." Spencer playfully grabbed the straps

of her bathrobe and yanked her toward him. He gave her another quick and gentle kiss. "I'll see you later."

"Bye," Cassie squeaked out. He walked down the stairs and waved.

A small cough caught her attention. She looked up.

At the top of the next stairwell, Daniel stared down at her.

Her heart dropped to her stomach.

Chapter 20

"*Al Capone*?" Lexy pulled her knees onto the sofa, sitting in the same spot Spencer had sat in less than an hour ago. "For real?"

"For real." Cassie was determined to think about the investigation and push the memory of Spencer's kiss out of her head. Now wasn't the time to think about that. And *never* was the time to think about the fact Daniel saw Spencer kiss her goodbye.

"According to the area history archives, the estate was built in 1927. The same year Capone started rebottling Canadian whiskey as his own." A wave of nausea surged through her stomach. Daniel had seen her kiss Spencer.

"And you really think ole Scarface owned it?"

Lexy examined the Old Log Cabin whiskey bottle.

"I don't know for sure, but it certainly makes sense. And gives a reason why the explosion was so close to the wall in the cellar. Someone was probably looking for a tunnel."

"Woah!" Lexy's eyes widened. "Do you think Al Capone could have a vault on the estate?"

"I think someone seems to believe so." As soon as she'd seen the pained look on Daniel's face, Cassie had shut the door, called Lexy, and asked her to come over immediately. Now that she was here, she couldn't bring herself to talk out loud about Daniel and Spencer. How could she convey feelings she couldn't even understand? Or the feelings she didn't want to face? She opted to fill Lexy in on the investigation instead.

"Maybe you can do a title search at the land registry office to verify it." Lexy placed the bottle back on the table.

"I thought about it, but do you really think Al Capone would've registered the house in his own name?"

"Good point." Lexy stared at the bottle. "It does make sense, but why murder Norma?"

Spencer had kissed her. "I'm not sure that was part of the plan. It was actually the fire that killed her, and it started by accident after the explosion."

"So, it wasn't murder?"

"More like manslaughter. I think that's what

the charge would be."

Lexy nodded. "Where do we go from here?"

"I want to stop in to see Mrs. Dingham and ask where she got the whiskey bottles. I thought that might be a good next move."

Lexy nodded. "Good idea. Grab your sweater. It's chilly."

Cassie couldn't deny the chill. It had been travelling up and down her spine ever since she'd seen the look on Daniel's face. "Okay. Let's go." She grabbed a brown hoodie and tugged her runners on without untying the laces.

Lexy slipped her feet into her furry boots. As she zipped her coat, Cassie stood in front of the closed door.

"What are you waiting for?"

Cassie hesitated a moment longer and forced herself to pull the knob. "Uh. Nothing." She looked up. Daniel was no longer there, of course, but Cassie still pictured him there. She quickly rushed down the stairs and out the side door, with Lexy chasing after her.

"I didn't mean you had to run!"

Once outside, Cassie immediately crossed the street and kept her line of sight straight ahead of her. She would *not* look back to see if Daniel was watching from the store window. And this time, she meant it.

"I mean it." Lexy panted as she caught up.

"What's gotten into you?"

"Nothing." Cassie continued her swift pace down the street to Mrs. Dingham's shop.

A couple of scarecrows in an old wooden wheelbarrow had been added to the display outside the antique store. The girls crossed the porch and entered the building, greeted by the sound of the ringing cowbells on the door.

"Cassie! You're back again." Mrs. Dingham set her knitting down on the counter and stood. Cassie swore she heard the old woman's bones creak in the process.

"Hi, Mrs. Dingham. Do you have any of those Old Log Cabin whiskey bottles left?"

She shuffled out from behind the counter. "You liked the one Spencer gave you, did you?" Mrs. Dingham grinned.

"Yes. Very much."

Cassie and Lexy followed the old woman through the maze of aisles to the bottle display. She bent to pull out an old wooden box from way underneath the table.

"Let me help you with that." Cassie reached forward to grab the edge of the crate.

"I'm fine." Mrs. Dingham lightly tapped Cassie's hand. "If I stop using my muscles, they'll disappear all together." She slid the box out to the floor in front of them. There was no lid, and it was filled with a number of other whiskey bottles. "Is this what you're looking for?"

Cassie grabbed one. "Yes. Exactly this."

"There's a bunch in here. Do you want them all?"

Cassie realized the woman hoped to make a sale today. Not wanting to disappoint, she rummaged through the box. Now that she knew what the bottles were, she could see the remnants of Canadian Club labels on some of them. She picked out two with their full Old Log Cabin labels still intact. "Just a couple for now, thank you."

"Anytime, dear."

The girls followed Mrs. Dingham as she scuffled back to the front.

Cassie set the bottles on the counter. "Do you remember where you got all those bottles from?"

Mrs. Dingham furrowed her brows, making more wrinkles on her forehead than Cassie thought possible. "Not off the top of my head. But let me check."

She disappeared behind the counter and emerged seconds later with a large ledger book, longer than she was wide. It landed on the counter with a thud, and a small cloud of dust floated into the air.

Cassie coughed, and gasped when Mrs. Dingham opened the book. It was full of handwritten lists of what must have been every item in the store. There were columns of dates, prices, and names. The old woman moved her bony finger down the page and a moment later tapped an entry. "Here it is. That's right. It was the tall Nordic woman, Gretchen Sanders."

"Who is she?" Lexy asked.

"She used to be the housekeeper at that estate that burned down. She'd been bringing a lot of stuff in here over the last month. Said the old lady gave it to her."

Lexy and Cassie exchanged glances.

"The housekeeper?" Cassie turned the book to examine the entry. Gretchen's name was repeated as the seller for over half a page of items. "Are you sure?"

"Positive." Mrs. Dingham shut the book. "Anything else?"

"No." Cassie fished some cash out of her purse. "You've been very helpful. Thank you."

"Anytime." She pushed a few buttons on the old cash register. Cassie smiled when the bell rang and the till opened. "That'll be eighteen dollars, please."

Cassie grabbed a twenty and a five from her wallet and handed them to her. "Keep the change."

"Aw. You're a dear." Mrs. Dingham placed the cash in the register and pushed the drawer shut. "And if you see Spencer, tell him I have some more records for him." She pointed under the counter.

"I will. Thanks!" Spencer had kissed her, and

Daniel had seen them together.

Cassie stepped out into the crisp air, hoping to push the thought out of her mind.

"The housekeeper!" Leaves crunched under Lexy's feet on the sidewalk. "Why didn't we think of her before?"

Cassie shrugged. "There was no reason to."

"But there is now. Do you think she's the one behind the stealing Carl the gardener accused Helen of?"

"It makes sense." Daniel's face flashed into Cassie's mind, and she cringed.

Lexy pulled out her phone and thumbed the screen as she walked. "She's on Facebook. Her profile isn't blocked." She showed the screen to Cassie.

Gretchen was indeed tall and Nordic, towering over most of the people in the photos with her. The slim woman looked to be in her late forties. Her straight blonde hair hung just above her shoulders.

Lexy took the phone back and used her thumb to scroll through the page. "Looks like she has a daughter about twenty years old or so. They have a small brown terrier."

"Anything else?" Cassie stared out at the locks. Daniel's store was coming up across the street, so she looked the other direction as they continued to walk.

His face appeared in her mind again. He'd looked so dejected. And why shouldn't he? She'd betrayed him. Or did she? If they were friends, it shouldn't have mattered. And really, he'd been overreacting all week. Hadn't he? Cassie frowned. That wasn't true. She'd hurt him, and it pained her to think about it. Would he ever speak to her again? Should he?

"She likes dogs," Lexy continued. "There are a few reposts of funny dog videos, but not much of anything other than that. It doesn't look like she posts very often. Let me check something else."

Cassie craned her neck to watch another squirrel climb a tree with an acorn in its mouth.

"She lives in the village over on Poplar Avenue."

"That's only a few blocks away."

"Want to keep walking and pay her a visit?" Lexy shoved her phone back into her pocket.

"Sure. Let's stop at the Snow Dragon to get an ice cream on the way." Cassie pointed as they reached the corner and the cross street came into view. The Book Nook snuck into the edge of her vision.

"Sounds good to me."

"Anything to keep my mind off Spencer's kiss and Daniel's face."

Lexy stopped and grabbed Cassie's arm. "*What?*"

Cassie smacked her own forehead. "Ugh. I didn't mean to say that out loud. I don't want to talk about it."

"Oh, yes you do!" Lexy put her hand on her hip. "Spill it, sister."

Another squirrel climbed a tree next to the sidewalk and chattered. "Look. Isn't it cute?"

"Nice try." Lexy playfully slapped Cassie's arm.

"Can we please keep going?" Cassie's heart palpitated. The bookstore loomed behind Lexy.

"I'm not moving until you start talking."

"Fine." Cassie sighed and slumped her shoulders. "But now I'm going to need a double-scooped cone."

Lexy grinned. "Let's go then. I'm all ears."

Cassie groaned. "Or a triple."

Chapter 21

Gretchen the housekeeper's home was a cute white storey-and-a-half house with a wraparound porch decorated with flowerpots with orange, yellow, and brown mums. Based on the wilted greenery in the numerous gardens, Gretchen's yard likely spent most of the summer in colourful bloom.

Cassie was relieved the trip had taken less than fifteen minutes. Between licks of her ice cream, she'd barely had enough time to tell Lexy the basics about Spencer's kisses and Daniel witnessing them. She wasn't too eager to go into details or answer any of the thousand questions Lexy was sure to have.

With Cassie close behind, Lexy sprang up the

two steps of the old porch and knocked on the wooden screen door. A dog barked.

The interior door opened, and a tall, blonde woman stared through the screen. "Yes?" A scruffy brown terrier stood at her ankles and growled.

"Are you Gretchen Sanders?" Cassie asked.

"I am. Who are you?"

"My name is Cassie, and this is Lexy." She held her hand out toward her friend. "I wondered if we could talk to you about your job at the Clarkson estate."

Gretchen's neck muscles flexed as she swallowed. "What about it?"

"May we come in?" Lexy asked.

"Uh..." She looked over her shoulder and then turned to the girls, darting her eyes back and forth between them. The dog continued to growl. "Are you with the police?"

"Not at all." Cassie shook her head. "Norma was a good friend of my grandmother's. Maybe you know her? Dorothy Merrick?"

Gretchen's shoulders relaxed, and a teeny smile appeared on her face. "Oh, yes. I know Mrs. Merrick." She stepped away from the door and pushed it open. "Back off, Riley." She gently shoved the dog backward with her foot. He stopped growling. "Come in. Would you like some tea or coffee?"

"No, thank you. We just had ice cream." Lexy

knelt and held her hand out to the dog. It sniffed her fingers, wagged its tail, and started to lick her. "Hey, cutie." Lexy scratched his ears.

The girls slipped their shoes off at the door and followed Gretchen past a narrow staircase into a small living room, the dog at their heels. She directed them to have a seat on a flowered loveseat while she sat opposite them in a wingback chair. The terrier lay on the floor beside her.

An old-fashioned wallpaper border wrapped the top of the plastered walls, and an oval rug covered the hardwood floors under the seventies-style coffee table in the middle of the room. Against the far wall, an upright piano stood, the top surface spread with various framed photos of Gretchen and a blonde girl.

"Is that your daughter?" Cassie asked, pointing at the photos. She recalled reading once that asking about people's children often put them at ease.

"Yes." Gretchen gave a full smile for the first time. "Nicole. She's away at college now, studying to be a nurse."

"You must be proud of her," Lexy added.

"She's done well. I'm a single mother, so it's been a bit of a struggle, but now she's an adult, pursuing her dream."

Cassie was glad to see Gretchen relax and open up. "It must have been difficult, raising her on your own."

"It was." She twisted her hands in her lap. "It still is."

"I'm sorry about Norma. It must have been difficult to lose the income, and then lose your friend too."

Gretchen's back stiffened. "Thank you. I'd known for a while the job was coming to an end, so it wasn't a shock. Unlike the fire and her death."

"So tragic," Cassie agreed. "Did you know it started with an explosion?"

"I heard that." Gretchen's cheek twitched, and she continued to wring her hands. "I don't know why Wesley would do such a thing. He was a bit strange, but he never struck me as someone who could commit such a horrible act."

Cassie leaned forward. "Oh, didn't you hear? Wesley didn't do it."

"Really?" Gretchen's eyes widened. "Then who did? What happened?"

"We don't know for certain, but there's an ongoing investigation." No need for her to know it wasn't the police conducting it.

"Will the police be coming here to ask me questions?" Gretchen swallowed again, and Cassie was sure her cheeks paled slightly. Lexy nudged Cassie's knee with her own.

"We're not sure. Is there anything you know about the fire that could help them?"

"No. I don't know anything about it."

"Nothing at all?" Lexy asked.

Gretchen shook her head and stared at the floor.

Cassie thought the woman had been rather quick to reply, but it didn't look like she was going to answer any other questions regarding the explosion. Time to try a different route. "Where are you working now?"

"I have other cleaning jobs, though the Clarkson estate was the main one. I've picked up one other client since then, but I'm still open to take on another." Gretchen stopped fidgeting by folding her hands in her lap. "What was it you wanted my help with?"

"Did you like working for Norma? It must have been great to be on the beautiful estate all the time." Lexy leaned into the sofa and crossed her legs.

"It was a nice home, yes. And she was a kind lady to work for."

"Did she pay you well?" Cassie stared at Gretchen's hands as her fingers fidgeted again.

Gretchen furrowed her brows. "She paid my going rate, not that I need to tell *you*." She stood. "Have I answered all your questions?"

"Actually, no." Cassie put her hand on Lexy's leg so she would stay seated with her.

Gretchen's eyes anxiously darted around the

room, and she sat down again. "Okay, but I don't have much time." She looked at the fitness tracker on her wrist.

"Going somewhere?" Lexy raised a brow.

"No. But I go to bed quite early. I clean an office building before it opens, so I have to be there at five in the morning."

"Okay, we'll keep it short." Cassie sat straighter. "I've been spending some time browsing at Mrs. Dingham's Antique Shop."

Now Gretchen's face *definitely* paled.

"She's had some really interesting items in there lately," Cassie continued. "Can you tell me about any of them?"

"Well, uh... Mrs. Clarkson had me drop off a number of items there over the last month as she sorted through her belongings at the estate."

"Oh, Norma told you to take them there?"

"Yes." Gretchen gave half of a shaky nod and wiggled her foot.

"That's interesting. Because when I helped Mrs. Dingham go through her ledger, I clearly saw your name listed as the seller beside a number of items, not Norma Clarkson's."

"No. I... Norma still received the money." She avoided eye contact. "I just signed on her behalf."

"I see. Then you won't mind if I double-check with Mrs. Dingham? And Wesley?"

Gretchen sank into her chair and covered her

face with her hands. "Oh! Please don't do that."

"You stole the items." Cassie inched forward on the sofa.

"Are you going to tell the police?" Gretchen's voice was squeaky.

"That depends. Tell us the truth."

"I did tell you the truth." Gretchen threw her hands up in exasperation. "I'm a single mother. Times have been really tough. And now with Nicole in college…" She shook her head. "She has a bit of an academic scholarship, and student loans, but I have to cover the rest." A tear slipped down her cheek. "I want to give her the best chance possible, but I can't afford it."

"So you stole things from Norma and sold them to Mrs. Dingham."

Gretchen nodded. "I'm so sorry!" She buried her face in her hands again. "I know it was horrible. I never thought I would do something like that."

"Did she know? Is that why you set the explosion?" Lexy asked.

"The explosion!" Gretchen gasped and sat up. "I didn't have anything to do with the explosion."

"Are you sure?" Cassie narrowed her eyes. "It seems to me if Norma found out and was about to tell the police, you'd have a very good reason to silence her."

"No! No! I would never do that to her."

"And a minute ago you admitted you never thought you'd steal. The line was already crossed, so why not go all the way?"

"Norma didn't even know I was stealing! All the antiques were being stored in an old shed. She was going to give them away, anyway. That's how I convinced myself it wouldn't matter." Long-faced, she looked back and forth between Cassie and Lexy. "You have to believe me! Please!"

Empathy tugged at Cassie's spirit. She rose from the sofa, knelt before Gretchen, and put her hand on the shaken woman's knee. "I'm sorry I frightened you. I do believe you. We believe you." She glanced back at Lexy, who nodded her head. "I can't imagine the sacrifices you must have made for your daughter. She's very lucky to have a mother who cares so much."

Gretchen wiped away a tear. "Are you going to tell the police?"

Cassie sighed. The woman did break the law. She couldn't excuse that, even if she fully understood the reasoning behind her actions. But there was also a time for mercy and grace. "You are guilty of stealing, and I need to tell Wesley. It'll be up to him if he wants to press charges or not. But with your permission, I'll also share your reasons. Wesley has a good heart. I'm sure he'll forgive you, if you ask."

"Thank you." Gretchen sniffed. "I really am

sorry. I've felt sick to my stomach about it ever since."

"Maybe Wesley will give you an opportunity to pay the money back over time." Lexy moved to the coffee table and sat on its edge.

Gretchen nodded. "I'd like to do that."

Cassie looked up at the forlorn woman and felt a prompting in her heart. It made her nervous, but she knew better than to disobey God's promptings. If He was nudging her, then there was a reason. She gulped and forced out the words. "Would it be okay if we prayed for you?"

A small smile creeped into the corners of Gretchen's mouth. "Really? You would do that for me?"

"Absolutely!" Lexy put her hand on Gretchen's other knee.

And for the next five minutes, Cassie and Lexy took turns praying for the housekeeper, Gretchen Sanders. They prayed for another cleaning job to come her way, for her daughter in school, for Wesley's understanding, and for peace to cover Gretchen's heart. They thanked God for his goodness and His mercy, and prayed He would make Himself known to Gretchen.

By the time they were done, Gretchen had tears streaming down her face. "Thank you, girls. Thank you so much! I haven't felt this at ease in a long time."

"Our God is a good God." Cassie rubbed Gretchen's knee. "And He'd love it if you took time to get to know Him better."

"Feel free to join us at church anytime." Lexy stood. "We go to Northwood Church, but there are plenty of other churches in town too."

"I think I might just do that." Gretchen rose to her feet, followed by Cassie. "Thank you again." She pulled Cassie into a hug and then gave one to Lexy.

Moments later, the girls were on the sidewalk, returning to Cassie's building.

"Well *that* didn't go as I expected!" Lexy grinned.

"Not at all."

"I'm glad she didn't cause the explosion. I really like her."

"Me too." Cassie frowned. "Of course, this also means we're down another suspect."

"True. I hadn't thought of that."

"I think I need to call it a night. When I get home, I want to crawl in my bed with Pumpkin and a good mystery."

"Is this your way of telling me I'm not invited to come up and find out more about Spencer and Daniel?" Lexy smirked.

"Exactly." Cassie grinned. And then the grin faded. She was absolutely exhausted after the lack of sleep last night and the long day she'd had.

But yet, she expected sleep would elude her.

Especially when the pained expression on Daniel's face filled her mind every time she closed her eyes.

Chapter 22

Cassie stretched her arms above her head, and her toes peeked out from underneath the granny square afghan. Pumpkin gave a short mew from her perch atop the back of the couch.

Sunday afternoon naps were the best. And Cassie had certainly needed one. As she had anticipated, the night had withheld sleep. It came in fits and spurts, but not at all in the form of the deep rest she'd needed.

Grams must have sensed how tired Cassie was, because all through their pre-church breakfast at the English-style Hardcastle Pub and Restaurant, she'd kept the conversation short and light. Usually, their time together gave Grams a chance to speak some of her many words of wisdom to

Cassie. And usually, Cassie welcomed it.

But today she was grateful not to have had the topic of her love life come up. They'd spoken briefly about Gretchen and the investigation, but even those sentences had been short and to the point.

The morning worsened when Cassie had arrived at church and Daniel was nowhere in sight. Throughout the service, Cassie had continually stared at the empty chair beside her, strongly feeling his absence there, as well as in her soul. She'd even craned her neck a few times, checking to see if he'd perhaps taken a seat in the back of the church instead.

But he wasn't there.

And it was her fault.

Had Daniel really only come to church the last few months to be with her? She refused to believe that. Even if it may have started that way, she'd seen Daniel grow more inquisitive about Christianity and Cassie's own relationship with God.

Nothing she did could ruin that. Right? She hoped that were true.

She sat up on the sofa, tugged at the elastic in her hair, and made her messy bun less messy. Then she sank into the back of the couch and reached over her shoulder to scratch Pumpkin's ears.

What should she do now? She desperately missed Daniel and wanted to talk to him, but what could she say? Would he even speak to her?

Maybe she should apologize. But had she done anything wrong? After all, she hadn't planned to kiss Spencer. So why did she feel so guilty?

And despite her original resistance to the idea, Spencer had grown on her. She'd be lying if she said she didn't like him. And she'd definitely enjoyed kissing him.

Cassie sighed and stared at the rose in the whiskey bottle on the coffee table in front of her. She touched one of the soft petals, and it fell to the table.

Figures.

Maybe this was like the story of Beauty and the Beast. Only she was the beast, and there were two handsome beauties.

The water in the bottle was low, so she brought it into the kitchen to refill it before more petals fell off. She held the bottle on an angle, being careful not to get the Canadian Club label wet.

Al Capone. Had he really held this bottle? If not him, then most certainly one of the men who worked for him. She was still positive Norma's murder had something to do with Scarface.

Of course! That could be her excuse to head downstairs and talk to Daniel. His store was open Sunday afternoons. She could ask him if he had any books about Al Capone.

Cassie changed out of the yoga pants and hoodie she'd put on after church and opted for beige pants and a grey sweater instead. She put her hair into a ponytail and threw on her jean jacket. As she slipped on her brown ankle boots, Pumpkin rubbed against her leg and meowed.

"Do you want to come and see Daniel, Pumpkin spice? I miss him too." The cat meowed again, nudged her leg, and attempted to hop with her two front feet, except none of her body left the floor. Instead, her furry belly swayed back and forth.

"Fluffy butt!" Cassie giggled and let the cat out of the apartment.

Pumpkin thumped down the stairs ahead of her and turned at the bottom to go to the bookstore instead of Olde Crow Primitives. She knew where they were going.

Cassie hesitated at the door to The Book Nook, almost feeling as if she needed to knock first. She shook the silly notion out of her head, took a deep breath, and entered.

A middle-aged woman stood in the middle of the store, taking a book from Daniel's hands. He was smiling and laughing until he looked up and saw Cassie. Then his face fell.

"Let me know if you need any more help."

"Thank you!" The woman ducked into a shelving nook to browse.

Daniel and Cassie locked eyes, neither one of them making a move to step closer to the other. Pumpkin broke the ice by skittering up to Daniel and rubbing against his leg.

He knelt and petted her. "Hey, Pumpkin."

Cassie gingerly approached, but Daniel kept his head down and focussed on the cat.

"Hi." She pushed the word out past the lump in her throat.

"Hey." He still avoided her gaze.

"I, uh. I'm sorry about what you saw yesterday."

Daniel finally looked up. His stare was hollow, and there were black circles under his eyes. "Sorry I saw? Or sorry it happened?"

"You know what I mean." Cassie shifted her weight from one foot to the other. "I didn't know he was going to kiss me... I didn't plan on it."

"Yeah, well." He glared. "Didn't look like you resisted much."

"Daniel—"

"Just forget it." He stood and waved his hand. "It's none of my business."

"Rowr!" Pumpkin protested as her petter ceased his duty.

"Is that all you came here to say?" He turned like he was about to walk away.

"Actually, can you help me?"

"With what?" He blinked slowly.

"I need some information on Al Capone. Do you have any books about him?"

Daniel headed into one of the book nooks and ran his finger along the books on a shelf. "Here. There's a few of them."

Cassie stepped in behind him and breathed in his scent of cinnamon and coffee. She tried to ignore the flutter in her stomach and the urge to wrap her arms around him and end the nonsense between them.

"Excuse me." The middle-aged lady waved from the nook across the aisle.

As Daniel squeezed by, Cassie watched his back. How could she fix their friendship? And was that all she really wanted? His nearness made her head spin.

Cassie forced herself to focus and flipped through the books about Al Capone. She chose two and brought them to the cash register. As she waited, she clutched the books to her chest and scanned the countertop. Paperwork, some unopened mail, Daniel's phone, and... a Bible?

Across from her, a book lay open. She spun it around. Definitely a Bible. And not *just* a Bible, but a Bible marked up with notes in the margins and verses underlined. She recognized Daniel's handwriting immediately.

Cassie stole a quick glance at Daniel. He was still actively involved in helping the other customer. She took the opportunity to thumb through the Bible.

Her stomach flipped again. Page after page was marked up and underlined.

By the looks of it, Daniel had been reading it for quite some time. She quickly turned back to the page it had been open to and spun the Bible around to its original position.

Another lump formed in her throat, and she attempted to swallow it.

The other lady lined up behind Cassie.

"You go ahead." Cassie stepped aside.

"You sure?"

Cassie nodded, and the lady obliged.

After the transaction finished, Cassie placed her own books on the counter. She noticed the Bible was now hidden under a stack of paper. "I missed you at church this morning."

Daniel tapped the computer screen. "I had some paperwork to catch up on."

"I see."

"That'll be twenty-one fifty."

"Rowr!" Pumpkin seemed to protest the price, but Cassie kept her mouth shut. Now wasn't the time to make a joke about a discount. In fact, she was pretty sure Daniel was making a statement by not giving her one, as he usually did.

"Okay." Cassie held her bank card to the payment terminal until it beeped.

Daniel ripped off the receipt and handed it to her. "Why the sudden interest in Capone?"

"I'm pretty sure the Clarkson estate used to be one of his hideouts. I think it's the motive behind the murder."

"Really?" His eyes widened. He opened his mouth then closed it again.

"I'm going to do a bit more research and probably head back out there this afternoon."

"Oh."

Oh? That's all he could say? She knew he wanted to say more, so why didn't he? Maybe she should ask him to come. Maybe she should try to talk to him a bit more.

The door opened, and a couple of older men entered the store. Daniel stepped away from Cassie and greeted them.

Or maybe she should leave and head to the estate on her own. Without him.

"C'mon, Pumpkin," she called. The cat came waddling out from behind the cash counter. Cassie walked to the hallway door and fought back the tears trying to form in her eyes.

"Cassie?"

She turned. Daniel had stepped away from the two gentlemen and leaned around the corner of a bookshelf to catch her eye.

"Yes?"

"Be careful." And he disappeared again.

Chapter 23

The large shed was darker than Cassie had remembered. Or maybe it was just that the afternoon weather had turned a bit dreary.

Her cell phone flashlight illuminated the contents as she searched through tote after tote, box after box. Cassie worked through the front totes rather quickly. Now that she had a better idea of what to look for, it was easy to bypass the hoards of dishes, knickknacks, and tools. She didn't want to ignore them altogether, however, in case there had been any old items pulled from the cellar relating to Al Capone.

Satisfied there was nothing of interest in the newer totes, Cassie moved deeper into the shed to search the older boxes and wooden crates. She panned the flashlight around the room. These ones had been here a while and contained more old tools and gardening supplies—probably also Norma's from the earlier years of her life.

She placed the phone so the light illuminated the area around her. She located the crate of Old Log Cabin whiskey bottles and rummaged through the only real evidence so far that this estate may have had something to do with Capone. Cassie pulled out five bottles and saw an old green army blanket underneath. As she unfolded it, a cloud of dust rose into the already dirty air.

Cassie waved her hand and coughed. There was nothing below the blanket. She sighed and replaced the contents into the crate.

Beside the bottles stood another wooden crate. This one had a sealed lid. Cassie squeezed her way back to the tools and searched until she found a claw hammer. Satisfied it would do the trick, she returned to the sealed crate and pried the lid open.

Nothing but old newspapers.

Her phone rang. Spencer's name flashed on the screen. She swiped the answer button. "Hi."

"Hey. How's it going?"

His gruff voice made her blush as she remembered their kiss. "Okay. I'm at the Clarkson estate poking through the boxes in the shed."

"Have you found anything?"

"Other than the whiskey bottles I spotted

before, no. Not yet."

"Do you want some help? Or company?"

Cassie stood and rested her elbow on a tall stack of crates. "Sure. If you're not busy." A cobweb floated in front of her face, and she brushed it away.

"I'm never too busy for you."

"Cute."

Spencer chuckled. "But true."

Cassie peered around the stack of crates. "Hang on a sec." She held out the phone, directing the light. Behind the stack sat an old wooden trunk with "U.S." and some numbers written on top. The dust on the lid had been disturbed, leaving two distinct handprints. The latch was unlocked.

She returned the phone to her ear. "I think I might have found something." She shimmied her way to it.

"What is it?"

"An old trunk of some kind. Someone's been in it recently." The hinged lid creaked as Cassie lifted it. "Just a minute. I need the flashlight again. I'll put you on speaker." She pointed the beam onto the contents.

"Tell me what you see."

She let the lid fall all the way open so she could use her free hand. "Looks like an old army uniform. There's also a razor, a toothbrush, old cigarettes, and some socks."

"Sounds like a military footlocker. Were there numbers on the lid?"

"Yes, and it said, 'U.S.'"

"Yup. Definitely a locker."

Cassie removed the top tray with the personal items, set it aside, and turned the phone light back into the footlocker.

"There are yellowish blocks underneath. And a bunch of wires and weird tube things."

"Cassie! Get out of there!" Spencer yelled.

Cassie moved one of the yellow blocks and stared at a worn paper label reading, "TNT." Beside that sat three grenades. "Oh my goodness! Grenades!"

"Don't touch them! Get out of the building, now!"

"I am! I am!" Cassie pushed her way past the piles of crates and totes until she emerged outside.

"I'm coming right over. Move away from the shed and wait for me. I'll be there in fifteen minutes."

"Okay."

Cassie walked out into the yard and tried to catch her breath. Was she far enough away from the shed? A car was parked behind it. Had it been there before? It didn't matter. She wasn't going back to move it.

She scanned the grounds. Down the slope, the river flowed past a dock. There would be a good place to wait for Spencer. As she walked, her body calmed, and her mind cleared.

A footlocker. And no doubt the TNT used in the cellar. She hoped she hadn't contaminated any fingerprints.

Did this evidence link to Harlan Waller? He'd know how to use the explosives, and she still didn't know if his alibi of being away at training was solid. But how would he have known the footlocker was there? It made more sense that the explosion had been set by someone who knew the estate. Her mind whirred as she walked.

Norma and Wesley. Definitely not them.

An image of Helen, the nurse, formed in her mind. She was fairly certain it wasn't her.

And then there was Gretchen the housekeeper. Cassie had no reason to believe it was her, either. Her gut told her Gretchen had been truthful with her and Lexy.

So, who else was there?

As Cassie approached the water's edge, she noticed an increase in the number of spots dug and refilled from removed trees.

And then it hit her.

Those weren't from removed trees! They were made by someone searching for something.

The same thing they were looking for when they caused the explosion.

A tunnel.

And one of Al Capone's vaults.

An image of Carl North popped into her mind.

Of course! How could she have been so blind?

Cassie whipped out her phone and texted Spencer. "It was the gardener! I'm sure of it. I'm walking by the river. Meet me here."

Spencer replied with a quick thumbs-up.

Carl North. Cassie shook her head, recalling the moment he'd overheard the girls claiming Wesley was innocent and someone else was the killer. He'd immediately added to their suspicions of Helen, accusing her of stealing, and doing his best to make her look guilty.

He must have thrown the brick through the store window too.

She reached the river and walked along the shore to the end of the yard. Beyond the cut grass and an old split rail fence sat a field with mixed trees and shrubs. Along the shore, more holes had been dug and refilled.

Had he found the tunnel?

Cassie jumped the fence and stomped through the field, pushing the tall strands of grass aside, reminding herself to check for ticks when she got home.

If there was a tunnel, it would've been used to hide liquor and to cart it from a large room or a vault to the river for easy transport. She followed the shore, staying a few feet inland from where the holes had been dug. A tunnel would likely have an opening right—

"Ah!" Cassie yelled as her feet fell out from beneath her and a mass of grass and dirt zipped by her face.

A sharp pain surged through her ankle. She winced.

It was dark, and she was sitting on cold, wet ground. The sky loomed far above her at the top of the dark shaft she'd fallen into.

Cassie fished her phone out of her back pocket and swiped the screen. "Ouch!" The cracked glass cut her finger, but the light came on. She swiped down from the top and turned on the flashlight.

To her left, a narrow passageway, lined with old brick and wood slats every few feet, sloped down toward the river. The walls bulged in a number of places, and the pressure of the earth had cracked a lot of bricks.

Water seeped between some of the cracks and ran down the wall, creating the mud she sat in and the pools of water farther down the slope. Vines and cobwebs stuck to various surfaces and crisscrossed the passageway.

In the other direction, the tunnel headed inland, still only about three feet wide. It was drier, with less vines, but just as many cobwebs. A couple of feet ahead of her, the bottom of an old bottle stuck out of the ground. She stretched out her arm and rocked the bottle back and forth until it popped out. There was no label, but it was the same shape as the Old Log Cabin whiskey bottles.

Apparently, she'd found Al Capone's secret tunnel.

"Cassie! Are you there?" A voice echoed down the shaft.

Thank God. "I'm down here!" She tried to stand but found she couldn't put pressure on her foot. "I think I sprained my ankle."

A shadow blocked the light at the top of the tunnel. "Found you."

She turned the flashlight upward.

It was Carl North.

And his grin didn't look friendly.

Chapter 24

Cassie hobbled away from the entry shaft and moved farther into the tunnel, frantically punching her finger at her phone screen, praying she'd have a signal.

"Cassie?"

"Help!" she screamed. "Help me! He's here!"

Carl North dropped through the shaft and landed beside her, nimbly landing on both feet with bent knees.

"He's in the tunnel! He's—"

The gardener reached her in three stealthy steps. He ripped the phone from her hand, threw it to the ground, and smashed it with his heel.

Cassie lunged into the darkness to get away, pain zapping through her ankle.

He grabbed her arm.

"Leave me alone!" She swung her free arm into the void, hoping to connect with something.

"Calm down!" He caught her arm in the air and grasped her other wrist as well. "I'm not going to hurt you."

She took shaky, furtive breaths and felt him let go. A second later, his phone flashlight lit the tunnel. Cassie cowered under his six-foot frame. Cobwebs licked the top of his scruffy hair.

"What are you going to do with me?" Her voice trembled.

"What do you mean? I'm here to help you."

Cassie studied his face in the shadows but couldn't quite make out his features. "You're going to get me out of here?"

"Sure. But first you need to help me. Let's explore. You first." He shoved her farther into the tunnel.

"Ow!" Cassie fell to the ground in a heap. "I can't walk on my ankle."

"Then you better start crawling."

She pulled herself up and used the wall to steady herself, recoiling at the cold brick and the thought of the creepy spiders probably nestling between the cracks.

"Stay twenty feet ahead of me, in case the tunnel collapses."

"But I can't see that far ahead." Cassie turned.

"Let me use your flashlight."

"Ha. Nice try. Get moving." He shoved her shoulder again, lightly this time, so she didn't fall over.

Cassie put as little weight on her ankle as possible, resorting to a hop and using the wall for balance, carefully monitoring where she placed each hand with the little light available. After about twelve hop-steps, she heard Carl slosh through the mud behind her.

The tunnel snaked its way underground, the mud floor drying and becoming hardened clay the farther in she went. In a few sections, the wall bulged so much she thought it was about to give way. Almost every few feet, the brick ceiling sagged, held up only by rotten slats of two-hundred-year-old wood, leaving a number of broken clay pieces on the ground she had to hop around.

Ahead, a partial cave-in had blocked the path with a four-foot-high pile of earth and rubble.

"Start clearing it," Carl ordered.

Cassie fell to her knees, dug her hands into the dirt, and pulled out half of a brick still intact. She whirled around and hurled it in Carl's direction.

"Hey!" He lunged for her. "Are you crazy?" He kicked her backside and pushed her into the pile of dirt. "Don't even think of trying that again."

"Looks just like the brick you put through my

window."

"Maybe you should have heeded my warning. Get back to digging."

"Or what? You'll kill me like you did Norma?" Cassie rolled onto her back and put her knees up, ready to kick with her good leg if he came any closer.

"That was an accident!"

"You blew up a house and watched it burn… by accident?" She carefully fondled the ground behind her, trying to find another brick.

"I'm not a murderer! I didn't know she was home! And the TNT was only supposed to blow a small hole in the wall, not take the whole place down." He waved his arm, making the beam of light whirl around the tight space.

"Tell that to Wesley! Speaking of which, when did you put the TNT residue in Wesley's trunk?"

"Clever one, aren't you? It was easy. As soon as I found out Norma was killed, I went back to the estate. People were there for hours, watching the fire and talking about the *tragedy*." He rolled his eyes. "Wesley had returned from the city by then, and when I heard the cops questioning him, I knew I had my scapegoat. No one in Banford locks their vehicles, including Wesley. With all the commotion, no one noticed me grab more TNT from the shed and wipe it across the bottom of Wesley's trunk."

"And all because you were looking for this tunnel?"

"Yes. And if I'd known you'd find it for me, I wouldn't have bothered with the TNT."

"How did you know to look for a tunnel in the first place?" Her stalling worked as she finally felt a rough-edged corner and carefully wrapped her fingers around the chunk of brick.

"I was searching for some gardening tools in the shed and came across a crate of Capone's whiskey bottles. Then when Norma asked me to grab some totes from the cellar, I saw the old wooden keg in the corner. I'd heard rumours of Capone being in the area, and I knew the house was old. It just made sense. There was bound to be a tunnel to connect to the river, and a storage room or a vault around."

Cassie used his moment of distraction to thrust herself forward and smash his knee with the brick.

"Argh!" Carl dropped his phone and grabbed his knee. "You stupid girl!"

The phone landed flashlight side up, giving Cassie the light she needed to make a second connection with the brick. This time, she hit his hand. If he hunkered down enough, she'd take a shot at his head too.

But she didn't have the chance. He fell forward and grabbed her wrists.

Cassie screamed as she wrestled the strong

man for the piece of brick.

She thrust her good leg out in a swift kick but only connected with air.

Carl wasn't there. He was being pulled backward.

"Get your hands off her!"

There was a smack and a grunt as two shadows scuffled. Cassie grabbed the phone and shone it directly at the two men wedged against each other in the narrow passageway.

Spencer held Carl by the scruff of his collar.

Carl swung his fist through the air, but Spencer caught it in his hand like a baseball and hit him with a right hook.

He threw Carl to the ground with a thud.

Through the dust in the air, Cassie could see Spencer pounce on top of her captor, digging his knee into his chest. Another swift punch to his face knocked him out cold.

"Cassie!" Spencer climbed over Carl to get to her. "Are you okay? Did he hurt you?"

"I'm okay." She wrapped her arms around Spencer's neck and let him pull her into him. She held on tightly, welcoming the safety of his embrace. "You found me. How did you find me?"

"I went to the river, like you said." He leaned back so he could see her face. "I didn't see you, but I followed a freshly trodden path through the long grass that led me to the shaft. After I jumped down,

I found your phone smashed. I knew right away what was going on." He put a curl behind her ear. "I ran down the tunnel and then heard you scream. Looks like I got here just in time."

Cassie squeezed him into a tight hug again. "Thank you." She sniffed.

He kissed her forehead. "You scared me half to death, Cassie Bridgestone."

She managed to give him half a smile. "Get me out of here?"

"Of course." Spencer helped her to her feet and steadied her as she struggled to keep her foot off the ground.

"I think I sprained my ankle."

He directed the flashlight down the tunnel. "It's too narrow in here to carry you. Can you climb on my back?"

"What about him?" She pointed to the heap that was Carl North.

Spencer looked at his phone. "No signal. We'll return for him later. If we don't decide to let the tunnel cave in, first."

He helped Cassie step over the limp body and squatted so she could climb on his back. She latched on, piggyback style, and held his phone so he could see ahead of them.

Spencer turned on a slight angle to keep her knees from scraping the brick walls. She buried her face into his long hair and inhaled the scent of sweet sweat and citrus shampoo.

When they reached the shaft, Spencer gently helped Cassie off his back and skillfully scaled the wall to the surface. Then he leaned into the hole with his hand extended.

"Can you reach?"

Cassie stretched her arm and connected with his fingertips. "Almost."

"Hop on your good leg."

She did, and he grasped her hand. With veins popping out in his forearm, Spencer lifted her out of the hole in one fell swoop.

They both sat in the long grass for a moment to rest before Spencer called 911. He gave them information about Carl North and was telling them about the old TNT in the military footlocker when she heard someone shout.

"Cassie!"

She pushed herself up out of the long grass to a standing position, careful not to put any weight on her sore ankle. Daniel, hands cupped around the edges of his mouth to amplify sound, called to her from the backyard.

"Over here!" She waved her hand.

When he saw her, he ran and shouted, "Are you okay? I got your call!"

"My call?"

"Yes. You yelled for help, and then the phone went dead." He leapt over the fence and pushed grass aside as he crossed the field.

She'd called Daniel?

"I remembered you'd said you were going to the estate, so I rushed over here as fast as I could. I'm so glad you're all right." He was close enough she could make out his ashen face.

Spencer finished his call and hopped to his feet. "Hey, Daniel. No need to worry." He put his arm around Cassie's shoulder "I saved her."

Daniel's mouth dropped open, and he froze in his tracks. "Oh." He ran his hand through his hair and looked out at the water. "Well the important thing is you're okay."

"Thank you for coming." Cassie caught his gaze and winced at the familiar hurt in Daniel's eyes.

"Of course. I'll always be there to help my friends." He turned to Spencer. "I guess you've got this, then?"

Spencer grinned. "Yes, I do."

"All right. Uh... see ya." He rubbed the back of his neck and turned to leave.

Cassie grimaced as Spencer picked her up and carried her. She loosely held on around his neck and stared at the back of Daniel's head.

Was she ready to let him walk out of her life?

A stabbing pain seized her heart, and it hurt more than her throbbing ankle.

Because that's what was happening.

Chapter 25

"Lexy was right. He *is* smoking hot." Maggie nudged Cassie's arm as she stood beside her in the kitchen, next to a stove full of cooking food.

"I told you!" Lexy grinned.

The three girls huddled together and peered underneath a row of cabinets. Spencer stood in front of the patio doors in the dining area, staring out at the yard as he talked on his phone.

Cassie groaned, adjusted her crutches, and lifted her wrapped ankle. She was thankful it wasn't broken, but a sprain was still painful. After a day like today, and then four hours in emergency, she had just wanted to curl up on her couch with Pumpkin. But Rick and Maggie had insisted the group of friends come over for a late dinner, and she had obliged.

Cassie couldn't help but think of last week's Thanksgiving dinner when Daniel was a guest. It seemed like a lifetime ago. How had things changed so quickly?

She was only just coming to terms with the fact she and Daniel might have become more than friends, and now she wasn't sure he was even in her life at all anymore.

But how serious could her feelings have really been for him, if she was here with Spencer now? Spencer, who loved God, who cared deeply for her, who had it all together, and was good, and loyal, and kind. Spencer, who had carried her to safety and had stayed by her side the whole time in the hospital.

He looked over and gave a wink. Maggie and Lexy unsuccessfully tried to stifle their giggles.

"Stop it," Cassie whispered and swatted at their hands.

"Your face is red again." Lexy snickered.

"I thought firemen were supposed to put out fires, not ignite them." Maggie elbowed Lexy, and they giggled some more.

"Please stop."

"I'm sorry, honey." Maggie put her arm around her sister-in-law. "We're only teasing."

"I need to sit."

"Let me help." Lexy followed Cassie into the

living room, placed some cushions on a chair, and pulled up a stool for Cassie to rest her ankle on. "How's that?"

"Good. Thank you."

Lexy sat on the edge of the stool beside Cassie's foot. "Are you okay with Spencer being here? Really?"

Cassie nodded. "I might not be here at all, if it wasn't for him."

"And Daniel?"

Cassie shrugged one shoulder. "I think that relationship has been damaged beyond repair."

Lexy patted Cassie's leg and gave her a sad smile. As Spencer approached, Lexy rose and headed to the kitchen.

"That was the fire marshal." Spencer shoved his phone in the pocket of his well-fitting jeans. "All the TNT and grenades have been safely removed from the site."

"Was it dangerous?"

"It was fairly stable, but you can never be certain with old explosives. And until they confirmed there was no dynamite with it, anything could have happened. That stuff can explode if you breathe on it wrong."

Cassie shivered. "And there I was, jostling the trunk around."

Spencer tilted his head to the side to make his hair fall out of his eyes. "But you're safe. And I couldn't be happier."

"What about the tunnel?"

"After they pulled Carl out, some of the guys brought in some safety equipment and dug through the caved-in portion. It wasn't very far to the house from there, and the rest of the tunnel was fairly intact until they reached the rubble from the explosion."

"No vault?"

Spencer shook his head. "It led to an underground staircase beneath what used to be the summer kitchen. As far as they can tell, it was only an escape route. Nothing more."

Cassie sighed. "All that, and a life taken, for nothing."

"At least you found out the truth, and Carl North is headed to prison, where he belongs."

Cassie breathed a sigh of relief. "I'm so glad it's over."

"So am I!" Wesley Clarkson entered the living room from the front hallway.

"Look who's joining us for dinner!" Rick followed.

"Thank you so much, Cassie." Wesley knelt before her on one knee and grasped her hand. "I'm eternally grateful."

"You're welcome." She pulled her hand back, hoping he wasn't planning to propose.

Spencer sat on the armrest and put his arm

around Cassie. "Hi, Wesley. I'm Spencer." He held out his hand.

"Uh, hi." Wesley accepted the handshake but winced as Spencer squeezed and narrowed his eyes.

Wesley immediately stood and backed away from Cassie. "And even though your heart was set on us, I don't think it's going to work out." He eyed Spencer. "Sorry to disappoint you, Cassie."

Lexy bounded out of the kitchen, covering Cassie's laugh. "You're here!" she squealed, wrapped her arms around Wesley's neck, and kissed him on the cheek.

Cassie stared at her friend, wide-eyed. When Lexy caught her eye, Cassie mouthed the words, "*That's* who you like?"

Lexy nodded, her cheeks turning a deep shade of pink, matching the shade of Wesley's. His mouth formed a schoolboy grin, and his eyes appeared even bigger through the lenses of his glasses than they normally did.

Cassie laughed. This day was increasingly interesting.

"Dinner is almost ready!" Maggie called from the kitchen.

Olivia and Lily ran screaming into the room.

"Calm down, you two." Rick gave them the dad-eye. "Just a quick meal for you and it's straight to bed."

"Aww!" the girls griped in unison but quickly sat in their chairs nonetheless, followed by the rest of the group gathering in their seats.

All through dinner, Cassie stared across the table in awe as Lexy and Wesley giggled and flirted their way through the meal. She shook her head. No wonder Lexy hadn't wanted to admit who her crush was earlier. Cassie made a mental note to tease her for the next six months straight.

On her own side of the table, she took note of how often Spencer's hand rested upon her knee during the meal. She remembered Daniel's touch under the same table recently. Both were gentle, both were loving, but only one made electricity shoot through her veins.

Spencer had a dot of mayonnaise on the side of his mouth, and Cassie reached up to wipe it away. He was a good man, and if this was who God had chosen for her, the electricity would grow over time.

"Thanks." His full lips formed a smile, and she remembered what it felt like to kiss them. To feel his five o'clock shadow gently scrape her chin. It was a good feeling, and she'd be lying if she said she didn't want it to happen again.

"And look what we have for dessert!" Maggie placed a deep-dish apple pie in the center of the table. "Grams dropped it off when she heard we were having a celebratory dinner."

"She didn't want to join us?" Rick asked.

"I tried to convince her, but she insisted the 'young people' have a night together."

"Oh, Grams!" Cassie laughed. "She's younger at heart than most of us." She didn't hesitate to take the first slice of the best pie in the world.

"What about me?" Spencer asked as Cassie stuck her fork into the caramelly goodness.

"You snooze, you lose!" She put a huge forkful of pie into her mouth for dramatic effect.

Spencer grabbed her plate with the rest of the pie.

"Hey! I'm injured, remember?"

"Yeah," Wesley piped up. "Give her back her plate. She saved me from jail!" Spencer raised an eyebrow and stared across the table at Wesley, who shrank down a bit in his seat. "If you want to, I mean. It's up to you, of course."

Everyone laughed, including Spencer, and then Wesley.

"By the way, Cassie." Wesley scooped ice cream onto his apple pie. "Rick filled me in on Gretchen and the thefts. I gave her a call on the way over here and assured her I won't press charges if she agrees to pay the money back by cleaning for me once a week."

"That's great news." Cassie beamed.

"Such a kind heart." Lexy batted her eyes at Wesley again.

Cassie rolled hers and smiled.

After dessert, Lexy, Maggie, Rick, and Wesley cleared the table and tackled the dishes, insisting Cassie and Spencer take a break.

At his suggestion, Spencer helped Cassie out onto the back deck. He'd wanted to sit on the porch swing, but she refused, pretending she needed to stand and stretch out her achy muscles. She wasn't about to tell him it was because she'd recently shared that spot with Daniel.

Instead, Spencer let her lean into him for support and wrapped an old quilt around them for added warmth. They stared out across the moonlit yard.

Daniel popped into her mind again. She sighed.

It was time to let him go. If Spencer was going to move into her heart, Daniel had to be removed first. It had to be this way, for her own sanity, and to be fair to Daniel.

She ignored the sudden emptiness she felt and turned her head to look into Spencer's eyes. The combination of the porch light and the moonlight added the familiar sparkle to his green eyes.

Spencer tightened his grip around her shoulders and kissed her cheek.

Cassie smiled and lifted her chin. He leaned in and softly touched his lips to hers, his long hair brushing against her face and creating a tickling sensation.

He moved directly in front of her then, pulling the quilt tightly around her and clutching it with both hands as he drew her close.

As Spencer kissed her again, Cassie thought of God's direction for her to wait. And how He'd spoken to her about Daniel and Spencer through the northern parula and the Lapland longspur. She'd waited for the parula, determined to find it and see the beautiful bird. She'd been so caught up with searching and waiting for it, she'd almost missed the longspur right in front of her.

And he was worth the wait. She knew it in her head.

In time, her heart would follow.

Eyes closed, Cassie enjoyed the lingering touch of Spencer's lips to her own, with her fingers on his chest feeling his heartbeat. Except for the chorus of the late fall crickets and the occasional loud bout of laughter from inside the house, there was no other sound.

Until she heard the buzzing.

And the chirping.

"Listen!" Cassie pulled away from Spencer and pointed.

Faintly, the sound of hundreds of migrating birds, way up in the night sky, showered down upon them.

"Can you hear it?" Cassie hopped on her good foot.

"Amazing!" Spencer turned Cassie so her back leaned against his chest, and he held her tightly against him. Together, they craned their necks to turn their ears skyward.

What Cassie wouldn't give to see the spectacle above her. Even so, hearing it was wonderful. She'd never before had the privilege of hearing a nighttime migration.

Bushes beside the deck moved, and buzzes grew louder.

A few fall warblers suddenly appeared in the branches of the cedar hedge, and one even hopped on the deck railing for a moment before moving on.

"Look!" Cassie whispered.

And then she saw it.

Staring at her, from the edge of the cedar, a blue-and-yellow bird sat still, unlike its travel mates. As if he wanted her to get a good look at him.

It was a northern parula.

PERIL OF THE BELLS
FAITH & FOILS COZY MYSTERY SERIES #3

Welcome to Christmas in Banford, where sleigh bells are jingling, cookies are scrumptious, and decorations are deadly...

Cassie Bridgestone adores Christmastime in Banford when crowds descend on the cozy village to visit its quaint shops, see the Christmas train, and enjoy the week-long festival. And this year will be extra special now that she's dating the gorgeous firefighter, Spencer.

But when she decides to help out the local food bank, she runs into her old flame, Daniel, and finds her heart torn in two all over again.

Then, one of the food bank volunteers is murdered. When Cassie is called upon to assist in the investigation, she has a hard time believing any of the kind-hearted workers could be involved.

Yet as she delves further into the mystery, Cassie finds herself embroiled in a far more sinister plot, with a killer willing to silence anyone to keep things secret.

Return to Banford for this Christmas caper in the third book from the Faith and Foils Cozy Mystery Series by Wendy Heuvel.

HAVE TEA WITH ME!

Thanks for reading this cozy mystery! I'd love to spend more time with you. Join me for tea?

Tea With Wendy is a newsletter I send out to friends where I share photos, life stories, a God Moment, book news and other fun stuff.

And when you sign up, you'll get a few FREE GIFTS!

I'd love to see you there! Sign up at:
wendyaddison.com/tea-with-wendy

READ OTHER BOOKS BY WENDY:

Visit: <u>wendyaddison.com/shop</u>

<u>Faith and Foils Cozy Mystery Series:</u>
(writing as Wendy Heuvel)

#1 – Fishers of Menace

#1.5 – Apple of my Die (FREE short story)

#2 – Ablazing Grace

#3 – Peril of the Bells

#4 – Faith, Rope, and Love

#5 – Pray Without Deceasing

<u>Devotionals:</u>
(writing as Wendy Addison)

God Moments: First Steps – 10 Devotions to Awaken and Grow Your Faith (FREE)

God Moments – Volume 1: 30 Devotions to Awaken and Grow Your Faith

ABOUT THE AUTHOR

Meet best-selling author Wendy Heuvel, the creative mind behind soul-stirring devotionals and faith-filled cozy mysteries, whose unique blend of faith, humour, and mystery will have you laughing, praying, and double-checking your locked doors.

Wendy has a life story that reads like an adventure novel. She's lived next door to a murderer, explored European castles, been a missionary in the jungles of Belize, and slept on the floor of a hut in the Sierra Madre. Her birdwatching escapades span over fifteen countries, and she's screamed at many spiders worldwide.

She lives nestled amidst the whispering trees of her 26-acre Canadian woodland retreat with her youngest of four exceptional children, fluffy dog, and mischievous feline companions who are always ready to lend a paw – or distract her with their antics.

Currently, Wendy can be found in her fairy tale décor office, watching British mysteries, or eating chocolate chip cookies.

So, grab a cozy blanket and a steaming mug of tea, and join Wendy on a journey where faith, humour, mystery, and occasional feline capers make every page an adventure worth savouring.

Sign up for the _Tea with Wendy_ newsletter for regular updates, stories and new God Moments:

wendyaddison.com/tea-with-wendy

FOLLOW WENDY:

wendyheuvelauthor

@wendyaddisonauthor

Wendy Addison

wendyaddisonauthor

wendyaddisoncom

DID YOU ENJOY THE BOOK?

Could you spare a minute and please leave an online REVIEW for *Ablazing Grace* at Amazon, Goodreads, or BookBub? It's the best thing you can do for an author, next to buying the book. Thanks!